I0623986

Star Siege

by

Mark Wayne Allen

Second Edition

Forward

There is at least one novel in all of us, or at least that's what I've heard people say. Well, I guess this is my book. It was written a while back and even published. I didn't much care for the manner it was published, but for a previously unpublished writer, it was my start into the world of professional writing. It has always been my desire to publish this novel in a manner more respective of the work that went into it. It is short by today's standard. The best known authors put down 200,000 words as easily as they breathe while I find difficulty just getting up in the morning.

It's a shame that we are all not evaluated by the standards of our own lives instead of having to compete against the aggregate standards of the entire world. Ah, but that would never work. It's not what have you done for me overall, it's what have you done for me today.

Everyone has bad ideas and good ideas. I think this body of work is a body of good ideas. Putting together a collection of even 40,000 words is not a task that you just say, I am going to do this as my project for today; it takes a concentrated effort over a lengthy period of time.

Ideas for story elements come from a lifetime of experiences and I really wish I could completely convey to everyone reading this that this is a work of fictional elements. The elements come from many places and, in fact, everyone and everything in my life experiences gets partial credit for where my ideas come from. A lot of things have happened in my life and these are the things that make me who I am. The reason for assembling these elements into book form is the pure enjoyment of readers.

I hope you enjoy this novel. It has been my passion for a long time.

DEDICATION

This book is dedicated to my daddy, mother, and granny in thankfulness for their steadfast support and belief in me: George Washington Allen III, Ellen Marie Allen, and Dolores McWilliams.

CHAPTER 1

He didn't know what hit him but he could feel the big knot on the back of his head that it left him with. He crawled dizzily to his feet moving gingerly so as not to antagonize the open wound. His vision slowly returning to normal focused on the forward viewscreen in sheer horror at what he beheld. It was a giant red star with it's bright surface spewing out flames across the heavens.

He tried to turn the ship away from what would be certain death, to no avail, the ship's controls were locked. Frantically, he searched the small semi-blurry control room for the switch that would override the automatic course plotting mechanism. He didn't intentionally overlook it at first, but he was in such a panic that it escaped him. After a few moments of calming himself down, he reached midways up on the control panel and pressed the bright red button marked 'Override'. The ship's computers electronic voice broke through the air thick with anticipation and said, "Course plot deactivated."

He moved over to the navigator's chair, gray with black upholstery, which was so hot it almost burned him, and tore at the wheel with all his might trying to alter the craft's trajectory. The ship's engines grinded with the power that was put to them and shook the ship, like his arms in their weakened condition shook the wheel. After a few minutes his sickly body gave out on him and he passed out from overwork.

When he awoke, he heard the ship alarms whaling in his ears and wondered whether he had regained conscientiousness just in time to die. The computer's semi-human voice ring out, "Severe heat damage. Unable to repair. Recommend abandon ship." Upon not seeing the red star filling the viewscreen, only the left side of it, he deduced that he must have altered the ship's course just enough to escape a certain death. He managed to get to his feet and headed toward the door and once through saw that he didn't have much time, the whole ship was steamy and ready to blow an air seal at any moment. His common sense told him that the escape pods would be

on one of the lower decks so he
hurriedly climbed down the half-cage
ladder and jumped to the floor as he
neared it.

The walls crowded in upon his
terror. Every wall seemed so close
that they would smother his skin with
the heat that was behind them. So
close, so close, he could not stand
the fear he was experiencing. He
slapped himself with his opened sweaty
hand to bring himself out from under
his panic.

His attempt to bring out from
under the spell of his panic had
succeeded because he saw another
ladder just a short ways from him
that, he supposed, led to a gangway.
He began racing down the ladder and
again jumped as he neared the bottom.
Once there, he began feeling of the
doors before he went through them
checking to see whether they were hot,
because he surely did not want to lose
his life by opening a doorway to the
stars.

After a few minutes of searching,
he found the escape pods. They were
metallic colored, round balls with a
big round viewport in the front for

maximum visibility. He knew he was lucky that it had not been burned too badly to use. Without hesitation, he stepped inside the pod from the rear seal, put on the spacesuit, and sealed the hatch. He sat down, strapped himself in, held on to the control board, and pushed the 'LAUNCH' button.

He knew that this was even a gamble because if the bay doors opened up on the side of the ship that was facing the sun he would die a very quick death. First, it would get extremely hot, so hot that it would cause the pod's air seals to bubble and melt. Second, he would, as a result, be exposed to zero atmosphere. It wouldn't be the worst way to die, but awful close to it. The worst part about it all, he thought, was his efforts to survive will have been in vain.

He watched the bottom of the pod door as it rose trying to catch a glimpse of the sun, if it was out there, trying to see if his worst fears had come true but was relieved to see only stars in front of him. When the door was fully open the escape thrusters in the pod sent him hurling towards vast, star filled,

openness while the ship exploded
behind him a few minutes later.

    In the pod there was food and
water for about two weeks at which
time he would starve to death. "Well"
he thought, "I'll probably see a nice
hospitable planet by that time." He
just hoped that the transmitter
worked. He looked on the right side of
a control panel filled with navigation
equipment and saw the black oblong box
with a data analyzer that was to be
both his friend and savior and tried
pushing the button that was to set it
in automatic mode. It did no good. His
heart and spirit sank.
    With the analyzer/transmitter
dead, he realized that he would
probably be in the pod a considerable
length of time, so he began trying to
triangulate his position with the
stars but it quickly became apparent
that he was unfamiliar with this star
group. Most of the stars were there,
Canopus was to his right, Lima was to
his left, but they were so
disorganized that who knows where he
was. His best bet was to venture on
hoping he would run into some shipping
lanes.

While journeying into uncharted
lands, he began to think about his
past, somehow he couldn't remember his
past. It was like he had just been
born. The more he thought about it the
more it drove him crazy. He didn't
come from this system that's for sure
because there were no habitable
planets in this system that he knew
of. But where did he come from? From
that ship? That seemed doubtful to
him, but he didn't know why it seemed
that way.

After four days, he was getting
very distraught and uncaring, he
thought he was surely going to die out
in space. He started keeping a daily
record of his thoughts on the audio
recorder in the pod to keep his
sanity. Talking to himself had not
been enough to keep his mind from
wandering to subjects that were too
depressing to think about. In his
journal of sorts he recorded things
such as his mental outlook, emotions,
events of the day (not that there were
many).

"Day 5, I am feeling silly today.
Maybe it's from having so much lack of
emotional contagion trapped inside me

and not having anyplace to vent it
except this recorder. I am growing
more skeptical about the chances of my
rescue each hour. I hope that no one
ever has to see me like this. Maybe
I'm being overly cynical, but it just
seems to me I'm beyond the boundaries
of the Alliance. I just wish there was
something to do besides sit and wait.
But, then again, I was never much for
. . ."

His dictation was interrupted by
the alarms on the ship that told of an
approaching craft. He had gotten so
busy with his dictation he hadn't
noticed a ship approaching. He didn't
fault himself though, ships were hard
to distinguish among the stars,
especially if they were far away.

Beginning to realize the true
importance of a non-functioning
transmitter he began cursing himself
for not trying to fix it over the many
days he had spent in the cramped pod.
Oh well, that was all beside the point
now, the best he could do was try to
fix it now. He fumbled with it a
second and remembered why he had not
attempted it before now. The screws
which held it in place were hexagon
screws. Hexagon screws had an inner

core of nitrogen complex which made them temperate when the screw was outside of a housing, because they are surrounded by warmth. But when put in a special type of screw shaft that radiates cold, the nitrogen takes over and makes the screw swell to the point where it took a Nitro-oxide wrench to remove them.

As the ship approached he could make out some details. The ship's hull was light-gray and it was very trim in the front. It then flared out to form a bulb-like protrusion. The hull tapered again behind the bulb and spread out to form the curved wings of a manta ray with heat ventilators in the midsection. There were two shuttle bay doors, that he could see, underneath each wing, hopefully one of which would eventually open to pull the escape pod inside. He couldn't see the tops of the wings but he knew what was up was a couple of gun turrets. But, curiously he wondered how he knew about the turrets.

After a several minutes, a transparent light-blue beam was projected from the forward side of the square bay door on the left wing and was directed toward the pod. Slowly the pod began moving towards the opening bay doors.

As the pod was seated on the x-marked landing pad, the bay doors closed and the pod bay hissed with the inflow of air. When it was fully pressurized a welcome committee entered the bay from the observation chamber.

Two men immediately started prying the door of the pod open. In a few moments, there was another hiss as the stale air in the pod rushed out and the pod door opened. "Captain Roberts sent me to meet you. He will see you shortly. I am here to escort you to the conference room where he will meet with you," said Commander Frank Doan. "Follow me please."

They began walking toward the inner folds of the ship which was very blandly shaded: light-gray mostly with some parts a tan color. On each corner of intersecting hallways there were colored signs apparently to indicate which sections of the ship you were in. On certain doors were the emblem of the space patrol which was composed of three diamond shapes, all attached at the center, with a circle around them. Occasionally at odd places along the walls were lighted indicators that had the numbers one through three on them whose use and meaning left him dumbfounded. Everyone he saw was busily jaunting from place to place.

When they reached the conference room, Captain Roberts and some of the department heads were already waiting on him. "Welcome aboard the Orion. I'm Captain Matthew Roberts. Please have a seat," said the dark, straight haired captain.

"Thank you. I suppose you'll want all the details of my calamity, but I'm terribly sorry to say that I don't remember much."

"We can download the duplicate memory discs from your pod to get a full account of what transpired but we would like to hear what you have to say," the stern, slightly wrinkled captain said.

"Yes, but after we're through I'd like a nice long rest in a quiet, comfortable spot somewhere," he said.

The middle-aged captain couldn't help but let a half-way smile rise to his face and said "I'm sure that can be arranged. Before we continue, what is your name?"

There was a long pause as he tried to remember and a hush fell over the room. "... I ... I'm not sure. It seems like I know but I can't recall. I tried very hard to remember while I was in the pod, but I just couldn't remember."

"Please, Think very hard once again. It's important that we know," said the captain.

There was another pause, longer than before. "I'm sorry, I just can't remember."

The captain's face changed from heavy concern to interest. "Well, we need something to call you. Pick a name you'd like to be called."

After a pause the man said, "Well I think I've always been fond of the name Ted."

"Alright, then Ted it is. Now Ted, tell us everything you can recall about how you came to be in the escape pod."

"Apparently I got a blow to the head by a falling object or something, when I awoke the first time I was in a scout ship, the name of which I'm unsure of, computer locked on a direct

course with a red star. After a few .
. ."

Helmsman James Rupart interrupted,
"Probably the sensors link to the
master computer had shorted out."

"If that's true, captain, the
pod's backup of the computer log will
need lots of work to be accurate. For
now, we'll have to depend almost
solely on our guests testimony," came
the voice of Science Officer Craig
Holt.

"That shouldn't prove to be any
problem. Please continue . . ." the
captain said with a hand gesture in
Ted's direction.

"After a few seconds of panic I
began searching for the override."
Beads of sweat were beginning to
spring forth on Ted's smooth skinned
forehead. Apparently unaware or not
acknowledging that anything was wrong
he continued with his tale. "Turned it
on, and tried with all my might to
alter the ships course. In a few brief
moments I passed out. I'm not sure how
long I was out, but when I awoke, I
had missed the star but the intense
heat had badly damaged the ship so I
... so I ... so I"

At that very instance he felt light-headed, dizzy, and after a few seconds passed out. The officers in the room, with the exception of James, had long since noticed something was wrong and rushed to his side.

Captain Roberts seeing that the other men had him securely in their grasp walked over to the intercom on far wall. "Emergency, medical team to the main conference room!"

CHAPTER 2

When the team of four men arrived, they were dressed in red jump-suits and wore red caps. They first ran a scanning bar about six inches over Ted's body which was elongated on the floor. The top of the bar had a silver strip in the middle and the bottom emitted a blue light.

As the bar moved an unemotional, unwavering, slightly monotone female voice rang out, "Massive infection from wound in rear of head, temperature (104?), blood pressure 160 over 92, accelerated heart rate. All other health factors in nominal ranges."

Upon hearing the analysis, the emergency technicians rushed Ted to Medtech. Doctor Lomar, the first to notice him wavering, attended to him immediately upon his arrival, knowing that any infection above the nose had no major body defense systems to contend with and would therefore infect the brain.

She took what measures she could,
then pumped Ted full of the strongest
antibiotic that was available, cleaned
up the wound and bandaged it, and then
transferred him to a bed via A-grav
units.

"I think I got to him in time but
we'll have to wait and see. If I got
to him in time, he should hopefully
wake up in a day or two," Doctor Lomar
said with a doubt in her voice.

"What are his chances of
recovering Doc," asked Captain
Roberts.

"Not too good. He must have had
quite a blow to the head. If this was
an accident, it was a bad one," said
Doctor Valerie Lomar.

"That could be very useful to know
if he makes it. Thanks for the
information. Keep me posted as to his
condition."

"Sure," the gloomy looking doctor
said.

Studying the error prone log tapes
from the pod was Craig Holt. His job
didn't seem particularly enjoyable for
anyone on board, except to another
science officer. Staring at equations,
theories, or in this case simply

trying to remove distortion from a log
tape was a tediously slow, drawn out
task, and Craig enjoyed every minute
of it. If any person was not
interested in facts or the relevance
of unknown sciences they didn't want
to have a career as a science officer.
All of his life, Craig enjoyed complex
puzzles, working with new electronics,
and all sorts of similar things.

He'd supposed at sometime in his
life that he'd been into most things,
although he knew that wasn't true.
Back when he was a small child he
played with building blocks a lot,
trying to see how many different ways
he could manipulate the blocks and
still end up with approximately the
same creature, device, building, or
whatever he happened to be
constructing at the time. When he was
trying to pick a career he reasoned
this to point toward engineering. The
fact that he had always liked and had
an interest in how machines worked
didn't hurt matters either.

Like many decisions that made his
life change, this one did so too. He
struggled through endless hours of
studying and tests, sweating every
answer, before finally deciding that

engineering was not for him. Although
a veritable fortune had been spent on
his education, Craig knew he couldn't
continue studying engineering.

So, once again he went down the
complex road of choosing a career. He
thought of things as psychology,
architect, and many others. When he
had run out of ideas and still wasn't
sure what he wanted to do with his
life, he decided to enlist in the
Areal Space Academy and let them
decide what he was best at.

The Academy was somewhat like the
armies of many countries on Earth in
the 20th century. It gave a person a
chance to explore one's abilities, in
this case, deep space, doing science
research, visiting alien worlds, or a
host of other things. Of course, there
were all sorts of other less glamorous
things like mining, fighting in wars,
etc., but Craig didn't care about
that. He just wanted to exercise his
full potential.

With the ship's log now in the
computer's memory, Craig tried an
equatorial filter first, because it
tried to balance the factual
information that the internal

recordings had correct and tried to reason out what happened outside the ship. 'Equatorial' thus meaning internal sensors equates to the external events. The equation in math looks like this:

(Real Events) = Internal sensors + (Actions of people ? Actions of computers * Inferred logic)

After he submitted the facts to the onboard Artificial Intelligence program he sat a few minutes thinking about his girlfriend in the computer room. They had been dating for quite some time and he hoped that as soon as their tour of duty was over they would get married. Her name was Jane Reaton and she had been an orphan until the time she was twelve, so she had a much different outlook on life than any girl he had ever met and it interested him. She had a tough, almost hostile attitude towards anyone, or anything, that displeased her, yet she was very tender and loving towards the people she cared for. It was precisely that kind of attitude that made her a good computer specialist. He knew with a stubborn, relentless attitude like that he could hand her any problem and she would find an answer.

When Craig finally rose out of the daze he was in, his job had come back and as he viewed the report he couldn't believe his eyes. The horrible combobulated mess didn't make much sense. "No, this can't be right," was his audible outcry of Craig as he peered at the ghastly log report.

He resubmitted the log using a different algorithm but to his astonishment it too came back with the same horrible mess. Craig worked at resubmitting the report with yet different equations, but with disjoint or nonsense reports. Finally, he revised an algorithm that he tried previously. The report that came back told an incredible tale. Craig let an audible gasp and was going to be damn sure this was right before he revealed the information. There was only two other possible answers, either it was the truth, or there was an error in either the onboard computer or the ship's computer.

It was too late in the work schedule for him to test the ship's computer, besides Jane was much better equipped than he to investigate a discrepancy and it was almost time to meet her for dinner.

Craig hurriedly went to his cabin to get ready for some valuable time with her. His cabin was similar to the rest of the crew's quarters. All cabins on the ship were somewhat similar with the exception of the junior officers. Their cabins were double bedded with a closet for each crew member. As for the senior officers, cabins consisted of a moderate size living area, a small bedroom, and a fair size entertainment area complete with table, terminal, and disc slot. Not bad, considering the ship had recreational facilities of its own, not to mention the many places to eat. The showers couldn't feasibly be water based, so the wonderful engineers dreamed up a sonic shower. A sonic shower bounces sound waves around in the chamber and breaks the dirt particles up. Not near as comfortable as water but it did the trick, once you got used to having your guts shaken. Once he was through with his shower, Craig dressed in formal attire for the rest of the evening.

The dress clothes worn on board ship were made out of the same satiny fabric, flutin, as the medics uniforms were, but instead of a red color they were all dark blue with a patch on the front, and a division patch. The pants were black and made out of the same material as the regular uniform. The contrast between the two turned out to be very pretty, even though the materials were quite different.

After quickly dressing, Craig grabbed a package that was on his bed and rushed out the door exclaiming, "I'd better not be late tonight!"

CHAPTER 3

On the bridge, Captain Roberts was fixing to turn into Matt Roberts and retire to his cabin for the evening when a communication came in.

The usually sturdy Melanie O'hara slightly shakily called out "Message coming in from Central Command, Captain."

"On the screen Lieutenant," Said Matt.

The large screen in the front section of the room lit up with the image of a man in his early 50's, gray hair, and medium build. The skin around his eyes was very wrinkled, especially in the corner and his expression was one that reflected the gravity of his statement.

"This is Admiral Rutherford calling the Orion."

A hush came over the room. Everyone knew that when Central Command called, they were going to go on a very big job. Melanie O'hara, the communications officer, always shook like a frightened cat whenever Central Command called. She didn't really know why, except maybe the fact that the job that killed her father had come from Central Command. She listened very close in her uneasiness.

"Go ahead Admiral," said Matt.

"An emergency situation has arisen at Delta Five. A band of criminals has captured the planet and are threatening to burn the Alphorzia deep in the mines there. As you may recall, Alphorzia is a very high yield energy source and is absolutely crucial to many planetary defense systems throughout the galaxy. Another problem is Delta Five's secondary industry, tourism. By closest estimates, there's almost fifty million tourists down there that are being held captive as well. The Aries and Centauri will meet you there as soon as possible. The three of you will work as a team to resolve the situation."

"What are their demands?"

"Guaranteed total control of Omega III and a certificate from the High Council of total and complete asylum."

"How big are the mines?"

"They're saying very big. The largest known, at present, but we really don't know. We just know it's the Alliance's principal source. Along with the Alphorzia are Diamonds, Emeralds, Sapphires, and many other precious stones in abundant supply. The planet is a virtual treasure house," Admiral Rutherford said.

"How numerous and how powerful are their forces?"

"We're uncertain as to the number of troops, but we do know that they claim to control all planetary defense systems. At this time we can not confirm that, however. Essentially our command center is blind, at present, and that means you'll have a hard job ahead of you," said the admiral in such a morbid way that Matt felt the pit of his stomach knot up.

Matt knew better than to press the issue further so he asked, "Can you send us any information on the layout of the planet and any possible weaponry?"

"All the information we have is being sent to you right now on a coded channel," said the Admiral.

"We'll do our best sir," said Matt.

"Good luck to you and your crew. Rutherford out."

The bridge was still and quite for a moment. Somehow the circular shape of the bridge seemed to resemble everyone's thoughts at that particular moment. There were questions of how difficult this would be in Pete Rupart's, the helmsman, mind. Yet, from people like Melanie and Scott Talby, the engineers, came thoughts directed toward the captain's chair. the captain would pull them all through with their help. The tension loosened a bit when Matt bellowed, "You heard it men. Mr. Kyan, plot a course towards Delta Five, Mr. Rupart, flank speed. There will no discussion of this, by any crew member, before the briefing tomorrow. Is that clear?"

Without pause came gentle voices of the bridge crew's answer to their commanding compatriot, "Yes sir."

Matt turned his head toward the right and said, "Ms. O'hara, when you receive the information from Central Command, encrypt it, then pipe it down to my quarters."

"Yes sir captain."

Matt knew that it would take them a few days to reach Delta Five even at flank speed, so there would be plenty of time to brief his staff members on the situation later, besides that it was late evening on the ship.

With that being his decision he decided to turn in for the night.

Getting up from his semi-comfortable chair he felt his feet bear up to his full weight. It surprised him that they ached from all the standing and walking that he had done that day; he thought he would have been more used to it. After entering the turbovator, he decided he would visit Valerie's office for something for his feet. After all, a good captain had to walk, hadn't he.

He knew it was a lame excuse to visit his confidant to discuss the upcoming meeting that he would undoubtedly call tomorrow, but he didn't care as long as he got in the door. He had become friends with Valerie in basic training. They helped each other study and became good friends along the way. Their relationship never did flower into romance though and it was something Matt regretted, but being just friends with a woman had its merits too.

He had gone in late to the academy because of his ill mother. They were not a poor family, but certainly not well off, and because his mother couldn't afford the treatment she needed, Matt stuck by her; caring for her the best he could. When he finally saw that he could fill his dreams and hers at the same time by joining the Space Patrol, he did. With his high pay in the patrol he could afford her treatment. He met Valerie in his first year there. Quickly, they became friends, but it never matured into romance.

If they had gotten romantic, he would have never accepted command of the Orion. It would have put such a strain on his mind, having that kind of a deep personal affection for a crewman who was just as subject to die as any other person. Matt always deeply regretted the loss of lives that were subject to his commands; up to a point. The point at which something impedes his operation of the ship, whether that be from orders he was following or anything else.

Matt beat her to the punch when the door opened.

"Hi Val. Have you got something for sore feet?"

Valerie really had other stuff to do but took a few steps back to let Matt in the door. "For you, sure. Come into my office," she said with a smile on her face.

Doctors' cabins were considerably larger than most because of having to treat injuries during the evening and night-time. For more serious cases, the patient was taken to the adjoining Medbay but with almost everyone off duty during the simulated night those cases were very few.

It wasn't really sensible to Matt to have just one doctor onboard but that's what Central Command decided right after he came to the Orion. Dr. Richard was one of lucky ones; he was sent to Angiola, a space station, to await assignment to a new ship that was under construction. The rest of the previously assigned doctors were either retired or making a living in private practice as best they could. Being a doctor wasn't good; especially considering the naturalist movement in recent years. The naturalist's would rather refuse medication and live out their lives drug free rather than introduce foreign chemicals into their body. A result of the ever increasing potency of drugs, both legal and illegal.

Valerie was a fairly young woman of twenty-eight with a very appealing frame for Matt's eyes. Her makeup was a bit brazen for duty onboard a police vessel but not to the point of distraction. She gave a body odor as if coated with the perfume she wore. She was very enticing, yet comforting to his eyes. Her light complexion reflected the florescent light but didn't seem to accentuate her small nose.

They went along with a minimal conversation until Matt's feet were soaking in a pan full of hot water with a little medicine thrown in.

"I know you. When you don't talk that means you've got something on your mind. Do you want to talk about it," Val asked.

"Yes," Matt said bluntly. "Another sticky situation has come up; this time on Delta Five. We're heading there right now. What's troubling about the whole thing is telling my senior officers about it tomorrow."

Valerie smiled as she turned her head to roll a strand of long blonde hair behind her. "You worry too much Matt. You do this every time a crisis comes up and you pull through every time. The thing for you to do is don't think about it."

"That's easy to say but not easy to do. When I look around the conference room I see all those eyes staring at me, waiting for the utterance of every word. Those are my friends in there as well as my shipmates. What if I get them killed," Matt said, displeased with her answer.

Valerie thought for a moment the recalled something she had heard in her college days. "Then you'll know that you made the decision that you thought was right at time and if you do that then you didn't make a mistake. As far their death, don't deal with trouble until your faced with it," Valerie wisely advised him.

"Well, I suppose that's true to a certain degree," Matt said judgingly.

Valerie knew she had him going in the right direction. Now was the time to set the trap. "Research every major decision carefully and think hard about the small ones. Treat every crewman as if you're giving orders to yourself," Valerie said without a shadow of doubt.

"That's nothing new; I do that every day."

Aha! He had took the bait that she had been so careful to dangle, like a juicy carrot, in front of his eyes. "Do you see? Just keep doing what you have done every day since your first command."

Matt looked at her with a slightly puzzled look and said, "Yeah, but that's different."

"How," she asked.

There was a short pause as Matt tried to think of an answer. "It just is."

A serious look was on Valerie's face now. "I'll tell you how it's different. You realize the importance of the situation whereas day to day operations are just minor things that crop up. The real trick is not think about the gravity of the situation and just go do your job."

Maybe you're right," he said as if convinced she had helped him a great deal. "By the way, how did you enjoy the hologram last night?"

"Not at all, My mind was on our space wanderer in the ward," she replied.

"Now who worries too much," Matt said.

She let out a minute laugh and showed her pearly white teeth, "I suppose you're right."

"How is our patient by the way," asked Matt of the shapely doctor.

"As well as could be expected I guess. His vital signs are still weak but at least they're steady," Valerie said.

"Well, I wish him luck."

"I was just about to have dinner when you arrived. Would you like to join me?"

"No thanks. I really better put this stuff away and get to my cabin and rest for tomorrow's meeting. Thank you for talking to me though," he said as he began to put the pan away.

"I just have a friendly ear, that's all," Valerie said.

"I'm glad you do."

"Bye Val."

"Goodbye comrade."

In the very dim nighttime halls, Matt began walking towards his cabin. It was very late on the ship with a minimum of personnel on duty. You could have almost touched the stillness of the night air. It was like danger lurked in the shadows of the night. Every corner seemed to foretell of distress.

Matt didn't like the night simulation aboard ship because being a ship's captain, he was trained to be aware of situations similar to it. He knew it was ridiculous but his training and survival instincts told him otherwise.

He was thankful when he reached his cabin. After he inserted his keycard, a whisk of night air sent gave an erotic tingle to his body. If he indulged himself now as late as it was, he thought it would exhaust him. Still, the urge kept nagging at him, but he had the strength, and presence of mind, to resist while he prepared a cold sonic shower.

As he stepped into the shower, the icy air from the metallic circulating fans on the ceiling cooled him down very rapidly. Matt had always enjoyed showers because the waves sort of washed away the day. A water shower was the best kind because it beat and massaged tired and sore muscles, but water was so preciously hard to find these days. Only two or three sources of water were known to exist in the explored galaxy. Pity. It was a great loss not to have the satisfaction and pleasure of water in everyone's daily lives. 'Oh well,' Matt thought, 'sound waves were a pretty good replacement.' The only disadvantage was that you had to use skin cream every day, in order to keep the skin from flaking.

When he stepped out of his shower, Matt got into his night clothes and, with his urges subdued, sat down on the hard backed chair in front of computer terminal and began looking at the information Melanie had transmitted there. It was a map of the area and the floor plan filed by the architects at the time the building was constructed. There were other things also detailed such as storm drains, wiring diagrams, etc.

Matt studied the plans for a long time before he copied the information on a round disc and then laid down on his gel filled mattress in the bedroom and drifted off to sleep.

In front of the entrance to the one of the shipboard restaurants, 'Monamie', Craig waited patiently to be seated alongside his girlfriend, Jane Reaton.

The blonde haired hostess came to him promptly and said, "Good evening sir. Table for one?"

Craig was startled for a moment, then upon recovering said, "No ma'am, I'm supposed to be meeting my girlfriend here. I don't see her though."

When his eyes finally caught her, he said to the hostess in a friendly voice, "There she is over there. Aurevoir madam."

When he got near enough to speak comfortably, he brought forward a gathering of roses in his left hand and some candy clutched in his right which he had bought in the ship's store on his way to meet her. Jane's full lips began smiling as she began to sparkle with joy as she saw the treasures Craig had brought.

"How sweet! You remembered," she said cheerfully.

Craig's face already showing his delight at pleasing her asked his adoring companion, "How could I forget the anniversary of when we met?" He meant it be a rhetorical question. She looked disconcerted and began to answer him, nevertheless.

"I just figured with as busy as you've been lately you would have forgot. I know how you get when you have a lot to do."

Craig looked at her with an awkward smile on his face and said, "No, I wouldn't forget our anniversary for anything, man or beast. You should know that."

"Forgive me, I'll know better next time," she concluded. "I have something for you too; would you like to see it?"

"Of course I would."

Jane reached down to her lap and grabbed a medium sized sphere on a small round base and set it on the table. "Here you go sweetie. Why don't you press the sensor?"

Craig stretched the light-blue sleeve of his dress shirt across the table anxiously to turn the crystalline looking orb on. The machine hummed for a second then came to life with a majestic brilliance that surpassed anything Craig had ever seen. There were planets, stars and blacks holes, on the left side was a pulsar growing and retracting, on the right was a whole galaxy spinning slowly around its center, suddenly a meteor came slowly traipsing across the three dimensional view and a tear trickled down from Craig's left eye.

"This is beautiful. Where did you find
it?"

"I got it when we docked with the
Epsilon. There was a high tech gift
shop there," replied Jane.

"It's breathtaking, thank you."

"You're welcome." With a big pause
Jane asked, "So how was your day?"

Craig shook out of his fascination
with the object and began to answer
her, "Fair, and yours?"

"About normal with the exception
of getting pissed off late in the
day."

"What about," he said with a
curious expression.

Jane's pleasant look turned to one
of disgust as she took a big sigh.
"Some ensign was goofing around and
messed up the main logic bank of the
whole system. I have never been so
reprehensive to a crewman in my life."

"That must have been why I got
such ludicrous results today," said
Craig chuckling slightly.

Curious as Jane was she asked,
"What results?"

Craig, not daring to fill her in
because of the condemning nature his
findings, said, "It's too strange to

even mention but it kind of caught me off guard, that's all."

"If it was so weird why won't you tell me?"

Craig thought for a moment and then cautiously answered, "Wait until I find out the truth then we'll have a big laugh over the whole thing."

A waiter came to their table and asked, "Are you ready to order sir?"

Jane nodded her head and Craig replied, "Yes we are."

CHAPTER 4

In Medtech among the slew of empty beds, lay Ted, the back of his head devoid of hair, wrapped in white bandages, and laying on a white circular pillow that prevented any pressure from hampering the healing of his wound. At the foot of his bed there was a digital computer console that relentlessly measured his vital signs and monitored his body, which tirelessly pumps fresh blood through his body. On the left side of his bed was a computer terminal whereby any patient could view some of the selections from the ship's library or read updated reports on the ship's current status and mission.

Ted began to open his eyes slowly, started to raise his head, but his body's weakened state soon taught him not to try. He could hear someone typing on a keyboard so he called out to him or her, "Who's there?"

The young, brunette with a pony tail, woman who was working at the console walked over to Ted saying, "Well good morning. I was wondering

when you would wake up. Do you
remember what happened yesterday?"

The handsome middle-aged Ted
replied, "All I remember is being in a
conference, and now I'm here."

"Well in the conference you passed
out from a large wound on the back of
your head, we don't know what caused
the wound yet. Do you?"

Ted thought for a moment to no
avail. The sympathetic nurse, seeing
Ted having difficulty remembering,
interrupted his thinking to reassure
him. "I wouldn't worry about it. It's
probably not important anyway. Is
there anything you need?"

With as best of a serious look as
he could manage Ted said, "Yes, is my
injury very serious?"

"I'm sorry but I'm not allowed to
discuss anyone's case without Dr.
Lomar's approval. I'm sorry but that's
standard policy. The doctor will be in
to see you in a short while. In the
meantime, you can use our bedside
terminals to catch up on the daily
news."

Ted, dissatisfied with the answer
he received, managed a small grimace
and then altered his approach. "You

can at least tell me your name, can't you?"

The woman giggled a little and quite coyly said, "Sure I can; my name is Polly."

"Well Polly, it's very nice to meet you. Have you been here long," he asked trying to go around her sense of duty.

Polly let her face show a smile and said, "I was transferred here about six months ago. Listen, I wish I could stay and talk for the rest of the day but I really have some work to finish. I'll come back later to check on you. Do you need anything else before I go?"

Ted, quite dismayed now, decided to try one last thing and replied, "Yes, May I have a small glass of water?"

"Sure," Polly said as she proceeded to take the clear glass that had been sitting at his bedside over to the sink on the right side of the room. She turned the right knob and the cold, clear water came rushing down to meet the glass like a waterfall hastily goes down to meet the river below. After the glass had been filled, Polly turned the knob

again and the water coming out of the
faucet stopped without even a drop of
error. She raised the glass to eye
level for a moment as if to see that
the tiny air bubbles weren't harmful,
then she walked back over to Ted's
bedside, pulled out a big U-shaped
straw and put it in the glass.

"That's an odd shaped straw,"
Craig said amazed at the shape.

Polly seemed quite quick to say,
"It makes it easier to drink while
lying fairly flat." She pressed a
button on one of the handrails and
Ted's upper body began to bend at his
waist, as if bending over. Ted thought
it odd that the movement made no
sound, not even a motor humming. When
he got to a height that Polly thought
safe, which was about 40 degrees she
let go of the button, which stopped
the bed from moving, and put the straw
in Ted's mouth.

Since Ted had learned his lesson
from his earlier attempt, he did not
try to lift his head. Instead, he let
Polly maneuver the straw to his mouth.
He did not drink much though, as he
had hoped the incident would mature
into a more fulfilling conversation.

From the bland colored doorway, in
the room where Polly came, walked
Doctor Valerie Lomar, Matt, and most
of the department heads into the room
where Ted and Polly were. Almost
single file they piled into the room,
several of them chit-chatting along
the way. They walked up to where Ted
was lying nonchalantly, as if without
anything to worry about.

Valerie looked at Ted and said,
"How are you today?"

"I'm weak and when I try to lift
my head I feel woozy. Other than that
I feel tired and weak," Ted replied.

"The weakness is probably partly
due to being cooped up in a life pod
for so long, but the more prominent
reason is your head wound," Valerie
said. She then went on to ask,
'Do you remember what happened
yesterday?"

Ted hesitantly replied, "Yes. I
was pulled into this ship and then
went to a debriefing. Once there I
guess I must have passed out."

Valerie was glad he remembered and
said, "That's exactly right. Do you
remember Captain Roberts and these
other gentleman?"

"I certainly d,; only I don't recall any of their names," Ted said.

"That's okay. I'm Doctor Lomar, to my left is Captain Matthew Roberts, but everybody abbreviates Matthew into Matt; beside him is Craig Holt our science officer; to Craig's right is our helmsman James Rupart; to his right is our engineer Scott Talby; to his right is Caroline Conrad from our physics department; and lastly Stacy Beamer from the ship's recording service," Doctor Lomar said, and then added, "Stacy is here to make certain that you won't have to tell your story more than once, unless something unforeseen turns up." Valerie then asked, "Do you feel up to answering a few questions?"

Looking with unsure eyes Ted answered, "If you think it's okay, sure."

Waving her hand toward the Captain, Valerie pleasingly said, "Captain, you may begin."

With a slight nod of the head that wrinkled his double chin, Matt looked at Ted and with his dark eyebrows, slightly wrinkled, showing his determination to get every detail that led to Ted's predicament. "Do you remember your name today?"

Ted gave a quizzical look and paused for a moment. Finally he said, "I'm afraid not."

The captain looked over at Valerie with his mouth tightened showing his definite dismay at Ted's reply and she returned his look with one of soft eyes that showed compassion and a smile. Matt knew from that look from his compatriot that their guest was in good hands. He then turned toward Ted again and said, "Doctor Lomar and our medical staff will soon try to recover your memory. Would you explain to us what you do remember about how you came to be here?"

Before Ted began to speak, he took a big breath as if getting slightly tired, then said, "The first thing I remember is waking up and discovering I was in a ship that was computer locked on a direct course for a red star and I was extremely close too. After a few moments I found the override and then tried to alter the ship's trajectory. After a few minutes, I guess I must have passed out. I'm not sure how long I was out, but when I woke up the ship had missed

the sun and I was very happy it did.
The only trouble now was that the ship
had sustained severe heat damage.
Well, I made my way to the life pods
as quickly as I could and in a few
days I ran into you people."

Matt was the first to speak. "Do
you remember what kind of ship you
were in?"

Ted thought for a moment about
lying, after all he knew no more about
these people than he did about
himself. What reason would there be
for them to lie to him. It was true,
he admitted to himself, that they
might have a justifiable reason to
omit certain information. They might
have excellent reasons for that.
However, so far they had treated him
with what might seem like undue haste,
such as not seeing to his medical
needs before carting him off to the
debriefing. "It seemed like a small
ship. Perhaps it was a scout ship or a
personal transport,"

Caroline Conrad, one of the many
fine physicist on board, asked, "If
you could remember anything about the
ship, it might help us classify the
ship? If we can establish that much it
may suggest why the directional

guidance system failed as well as assist in answering other questions."

Ted's hand twitched a little before he could answer. "I really was too busy looking for the escape pod to notice any details. I mean the ship was big enough to have a gangway, but as for other details, I'm afraid I'm at a loss."

Scott's eyes were very soft as if looking at his best friend who was ill in the bed of his death. Nevertheless, he knew he had a job to do and began asking questions. "Did you notice anything strange, writing on the doors, or perhaps colored lines on the floor or any other marking?"

"I do remember a lack of writing on the doors. Maybe it was a pleasure vehicle. Oh, and there were stairs, the vertical kind with outstretches that came halfway around me as I climbed," Ted said.

Scott quickly said, "Those kind of stairs are uncommon captain. It should be fairly easy to match them with a specific type of craft," looking at Craig who had gotten caught in a daze thinking about his computer findings from the day before. Craig felt badly about his findings, but not too much so.

Trying to make up for his error Craig said, "I can run the factors we discuss through the computer and come up with a list of possible ship designs." Now that was in Craig's field and he knew it.

Matt reached up with his right hand to push his dark hair to the left side of his head only to discover the strands of hair that he thought were bothering him were already in place and that it was his scalp that was itching. He reached up with his right hand, scratched a little at the spot, and went on. "Very well Craig, see to it." Matt had not been too bothered though not to notice Craig's failing. He knew his crew inside and out, even though he did not personally associate with each and every one, and wondered what was bothering Craig. Matt continued, "Do you remember anything else that might help us?"

Ted gave a blank expression and replied, "No, I'm afraid not. But if I do, I'll sure tell you."

"Very well then," the stern captain said.

Matt and his compatriots, with the exception of Valerie, proceeded to leave the room as swiftly as when they came. Valerie stayed to begin the task of assigning someone to Ted's case.

The side door of Medbay opened as Polly entered the room. With purposeful steps she began walking toward Ted's bed. "Hi Doctor," she said as she walked by Valerie reviewing a medical personnel list.

"Hello," Valerie said as she began watching Polly check the readouts of the instruments on Ted's bed who had already fallen asleep. Valerie knew that it would take a diligent person to work with Ted and although Polly had been a bit uncontrollable in the past, but she was very thorough. Her headstrong attitude might well be an asset if the situation were handled correctly. The important responsibility of another person's fate, Valerie thought, might be exactly what Polly needed.

As Valerie thought, Polly finished reading the instruments at the foot of Ted's bed and began to walk back to her cubicle. Valerie walked up to her saying, "Polly, would you come into my office for a moment.

"Sure," Polly said as she began following Valerie.

Valerie's office was an offshoot of the Medbay main office. Valerie's room was actually attached to her office in Medbay by an adjoining door which could be voice locked. Valerie had never resorted to the voice lock but knew how it operated. She just never saw the need to use it.

Her office was rather bland but she liked it. The walls were a metallic light blue and the small wood colored desk was against one of the walls with a brown swiveling chair beside it. A crème colored plain chair beside the desk. The walls were bare except for a lone picture of her mom and dad. There was very little on her desk besides her computer terminal and a memo pad attached to her calendar.

Once they were both inside, Valerie sat down in her chair and invited Polly to do the same. "Well Polly, I guess you're wondering what this meeting is about?"

Polly gave a quizzical look and said, "I was kind of wondering."

"Well, don't be alarmed this is just, sort of an informational meeting."

"Okay," Polly said uncertainly. She knew she had had lots of trouble controlling her frisky nature and was afraid it might have caught her in trouble again.

Uneasy or not, Valerie decided to continue, "By now you're bound to be well acquainted with our visitor's condition. He's had a lot of trouble with his memory, as well as with his physical recuperation from that blow to his head."

"Yes ma'am I am. He's got a long road to travel to regain his memory, if he ever does. I've had a great deal of training in matters like this."

Valerie widened her eyes in amazement. "Let's see how much you have," she said as she turned herself towards her terminal. With repeated keystrokes on her keyboard, Valerie brought up on the digitized terminal Polly's record. It detailed a few courses in medicine and psychology that dealt with such issues as memory but the training was modest.

Valerie turned back around to face Polly and said, "Don't over estimate what you've learned Polly. The knowledge you have is valuable but does not entail the full story on memory conditions or ailments."

"I'll try not to," Polly said in unbelieving tone.

Valerie couldn't help trying to listen for that kind of reaction from Polly. "I'm serious Polly; there's a wealth of knowledge that you don't possess. If you like, you can access the knowledge bank in the computer."

"All right, maybe I will," Polly replied in an unwavering voice.

"It won't be long before Ted will need help in that area. I'd like you to work with him, if you don't have any objections?"

"I'd like that very much," Polly said smiling.

Valerie said, "There will also be a slight pay increase, temporarily at least."

"That'll be great, Doctor Lomar. Thank you for the opportunity," Polly said as she stood up straightening her white uniform along the way.

"You're welcome Polly. Now, I believe I've kept you from your duties long enough," Valerie said.

As Polly got up from her stiff backed dark blue chair, a short man with an equipment case clutched in right hand stepped into the office. "Excuse me ladies, but I'm here to do an identity check on the patient called Ted."

Valerie rose from her chair asking, "By whose orders?"

Surprised, the young, brown haired man said, "The captain ordered it earlier today. You mean you didn't know?"

"No, but it seems practical that he would order it. We just didn't discuss. Would you mind waiting outside for just a second while I check with him?"

"Not at all, miss, but don't take too long. I have a schedule to keep."

"It won't take but a minute," Valerie said. Polly and the short man walked into Medbay and began talking.

Valerie, on the other hand, sat back down in her cushiony chair and pushed the intercom button on her desk. "Calling the captain."

In a few moments Matt's voice rang out through the intercom, "Yes doctor..."

"Did you order an identity scan on our visitor? If so, may I ask why?"

"Yes I did and the reason is, I don't like dealing with unknowns. Unknowns invite danger," Matt answered in an inhospitable tone.

"Okay, Matt. I just wanted to make sure," Valerie replied, agitated by the fact that Matt had not previously discussed the decision with her. She then got up from her chair and walked toward the door.

As she entered Medbay, she looked at the technician who promptly got quiet, and said, "All right, you may proceed. I don't believe I caught your name though?"

"Henry Thompson, ma'am," the man said. He then proceeded down the adjoining corridor of Medbay to the ward where Ted was. He, naturally, entered the ward, followed by Polly who was swept up in curiosity, and walked toward bed where Ted was lying.

Henry began introducing himself as he began to set up his equipment. "I am Henry Thompson and I have been assigned to do an identity check on you sir." He pulled a tabletop out from the slot that was below the mattress and set the luminous gray equipment case onto the hideaway table.

Ted gave the stuffy, short man a queer look, mumbled a few sounds representing indecision, and then finally said, "Okay Mr. Thompson. Frankly I'll be glad when all the confusion is over."

"Fine, fine, well it'll all be over in a minute," Henry said, as he opened the case. He then looked over at Polly and said, "Nurse, for this to be effective, it will require that the lighting be dim and we will need privacy."

"Yes sir. I'll dim the lights on my way out," Polly said. She then walked over to the exiting doorway that led to the Medbay corridor and turned a knob. The lights in the ward went dim and then Polly stepped out of the doorway and pulled a fan-fold vertical shade behind her to cover the doorway.

Henry, who was already fiddling with the dials inside the case, replied, "Thank you, miss." He then got a small tabletop with fold-out legs from the case, and proceeded to fold out the legs and set it on the bed so that it was setting above Ted's groin. Ted saw the man then remove two hand size plates with wires attached from the case. Henry sat the plates on the tabletop. "Would you put your hands on the plates sir."

Ted, removing his hands from below the cover, did as man had said to do. The plates were cold when he touched them and he immediately withdrew his hands and said, "... cold ...," in a shuddery voice.

"I'm sorry Mr. Ted, but the plates are necessary," Henry said without sympathy.

As Ted slowly coaxed his hand to touch the cold things, Henry took what looked like a pair of goggles out of the case. "Now sir, I'm going to have to put this headset over your eyes." He was proceeding to get up when Ted's voice distracted him.

"Mr. Thompson, I'd like to ask what the headset is for?"

"Each person has a separate ultra-high frequency that their brain works off of. This headset," Henry said as he patted the black goggles, "will monitor your brain activity and thereby register your individual frequency. The hand plates assist the machine."

Ted, with wide eyes, arched his back, as if from discomfort, then said, "Okay, doc."

As all the department heads piled into the briefing room, as the captain had ordered them to the night before, there was a naturally calm look on everyone's faces. Several were standing in one corner swapping jokes. The room was very big and had a large, round, white table in the center. It's surface was smooth except for a bland colored orb in the center and a panel with buttons in front of one of the chairs. The light gray walls were sectioned, about four feet per section, with a one inch notch between each section.

When Matt came in a hush came over the room and everyone quickly took their seat. Matt circled around the table and headed for the vacant seat. When he got there he remained standing and started the conference by saying, "Good day everyone."

Continuing he said, "People, we have a tricky situation on Delta Five, as we all know. Our handling of that situation is of extreme intergalactic importance. Not only does it have major consequences for this system, but this galaxy and other galaxies will suffer too if the Alphorizia mines get ignited. Greatly! You all should know our tactical commander, Ben Waters. Mister Waters before you start your report would you mind explaining why The Pak and Cartier didn't just capture Omega III?"

With his blonde hair fluttering, as he stood up, Ben began by saying, "Well sir, although Omega III is ultimately controlled by the Alliance, they are governed by a military republic. By capturing Delta Five, which is directly controlled by our alliance, a non-military republic, they can avoid the military confrontation that would take place on Omega III."

"Now for the briefing. The situation is a bit tricky, but we can accomplish our task." Ben stressed the word, 'can', because he felt the hostage situation was problematic. He continued by saying, "Obviously, the bandit's dealings will be with you, captain. We can use that to our advantage. We can plant a new camera transceiver that we just developed on you. That way we'll get a panoramic view of the situation, and thus it will be easier to devise an easy entry, should we decide to try to militarily overturn the captures." Ben shifted positions as he completed his point.

"The original layout of the political installation is complex and heavily fortified. The captures have about 750 people protecting the capitol building which they are controlling. They are armed with Series 7 Pulse Rifles, which are very accurate and can inflict heavy damage, even compared to our Mark V's. They are very powerful!"

Ben pressed a button on the panel before him and a holographic projection filled the area just above the table top. "Ladies and gentleman, this hologram reflects the original layout of the capitol building." Wincing a tad, Ben continued, "As far as we know, there have been no modifications made to this layout, but local politicians are not in the habit of communicating minor details such as that. Even if they did tell the local authorities about any modifications, the local authorities are also in this building. The rationale at the time of construction was that it would save costs." Ben chuckled a little, "It looks like they outsmarted themselves."

Pointing to the hologram above the crystalline orb Ben said, "Troops are heavily fortified around the presidential chambers and the documents room, where the current floor plan to the building is stored." With sort of a mild grimace, Ben said, "It looks like they knew we would be anxious to get the current floor plan. We can map the building with an ultra phasic snapshot from one of the weather satellites in orbit. The only problem with this is metal disrupts the ultra phasic waves and it will have very low power, given this equipment was never meant for this purpose. If we're lucky, they won't think of jamming."

"The leader of these band of criminals is Joseph Cartier. He's the former director of our beloved Crystal Alliance. He was released by our alliance when his views on the cohersed rebellion by The Pak's were thought to be interfering with his judgment. He underwent a psychiatric evaluation shortly after, at the request of the alliance and was found to be mentally unstable and a danger to himself and others. Unfortunately he escaped from a military installation en route to a psychiatric facility."

"This is an extremely clever man with a vast amount of knowledge about The Crystal Alliance. He knows our policies concerning rebellions, and he knows The Pak organization very well. He is very unstable and deviously clever."

"Luther Fen, the leader of The Pak, is the best of friends with Cartier. The pair make an awesome combination because they're almost exact opposites in terms of personal style and strengths. I believe we can use misdirection on them both though. For instance, we might let them find an active listening device, or two, while concealing another."

Ben took a moment to re-moisten his dry mouth. He reached for the glass of water that was on the table and took a drink from it. Setting the glass down, he continued, "In monitoring transmissions from Delta Five, we noticed a coded message that was directed toward somewhere near

Gamma Two, but there is nothing we can detect at that precise location. We think this may be a ruse, but we're investigating it anyway."

"We don't as yet know anything about what kind of 'real' threat they have on the Alphorzia. Long range scanners have indicated no potential threat. The mines are a hell of a long way from the complex they're stationed at, we have no knowledge of them being elsewhere, and the mines, as far as we know, don't go under the complex. That kind of gap in knowledge invites danger. We'll definitely keep working on it."

"The tourists, we feel, other than their inconvenience and the loss of revenue for the economy, will not be a major factor. They're not being held or threatened in any way that we know of. They'll be an inconvenience when dealing with captures, but not a major detriment."

Ben finished his chorus of information by saying, "The people we're dealing with are diabolically clever. Regardless how we go about it, dealing with them is going to be difficult. I believe we will succeed though."

Ben sank down into the stiff backed conference chair as if he was dropping a ton of lead and there was a long pause afterward. The tension that everyone was feeling at that exact moment was intolerably deafening.

Not a sound came from the room until Matt finally cut the thick air of tension with his raspy statement, "Opinions people?"

CHAPTER 5

It was early morning on board the Orion, police vessel of the stars, and Jane Reaton was busy checking her lovable computers for error. She was running the most thorough diagnostic program she had ever seen. It had full rhythmic logic testing and calibration. The rhythmic logic banks checks to see if electrical synapse's were functioning in the correct timing with the logic unit. The program could measure exactly what a person wanted by program definition variables.

In her absent minded curiosity about the foul play that Craig had indicated the previous night, Jane was having to rerun the program several times because she kept using the wrong definition variables. It aggravated her very much and that just made the situation worse.

She had had a horrible night of sleep. Tossing and turning and sleep deprivation did not usually combine for a good work day. She knew the computer systems like the back of her hands, but today nothing had gone right for her. Everything she touched

had turned into a mess and that made
her agitated.

This state of confusion went on
for a long time, until, finally, one
of the other computer techs said,
"Jane, can I give you a hand?"

"Yes, I've looked at this so much
that I can't hardly see straight," a
frustrated Jane said. "I'm trying to
run a full test on the overall logic
circuits of the science computer
banks."

"Well, that's a little advanced
for me, but together I'm sure we can
solve it. Hmmmmmmmmmmm....," the ensign
said, then paused a moment to check
with his terminal. His eyes darted
back up at Jane's terminal. He looked
up at the control panel in front of
him, studied it for a minute with all
of its digital and chronological
displays, then said, "Let's see …"

Frustrated by the tech's slowness,
Jane said, "Would it be 1 code=2
code2=5 3 7 1?"

The tech said, "Not quite. I think
if you say, 1 code=2 code2=5 3 7 0,
that will get you there. What do think
about that?"

Jane, with a giant size smile on face, said, "That's it! Thank you so much for your help Jeff."

"No problem. Anytime."

After saying her thanks, Jane keyed the codes the ensign had given her on the panel before her. After a long wait, she breathed a heavy sigh of relief when the program configuration came back with the results she was after. Although, these results weren't exactly what she had expected.

She knew Craig; it was not like him to hold anything back from her, as he did last night at the restaurant. She knew that since he held his comments about his findings, the news must have been dreadful. Telling Craig the results might set off a chain reaction that she would rather not be involved in.

Later that day, during a mid-morning errand run, Jane stopped by Craig's station on the bridge. The bridge was slowly sputtering with activity, just like Jane. Most of the bridge specialists were either working with their respective departments that were researching the hostage situation, or coordinating their

department with other departments.
About the only officers on the bridge
were Craig and the bare essential
bridge staff: Melanie, Pete, and
James. There were very few people
otherwise.

The desolation of the bridge
brought an eerie feeling to Jane. The
feeling was intensified as a cold
chill traveled up her spine. The
feeling that something horrible was
going to happen at Delta Five creeped
into her thoughts. As she approached
the normalcy of confronting Craig, yet
again, the feeling slowly dissipated.
Barely able to regain her composure as
she walked, she came up to Craig from
behind.

Meanwhile, Craig was busily doing
some telemetry computations at his
light illuminated post and didn't
notice his girlfriend slink up by his
side.

"Good morning Craig."

Craig was startled out of his daze
rather abruptly by her statement. "Oh,
good morning, gal of mine. What can I
do for you?"

Jane managed to crack a half-
smile. It quickly faded into
nothingness as she began to speak.

"I've got the tests results of the comprehensive logic test of the science computer that you wanted."

Craig smiled very big showing his perfectly white and straight teeth. It covered almost his entire face. Craig figured for once he had caught his perfect little gal pal in a legendary computer mistake. "And what were the results dear?"

Jane knew there was but one way to address news like this but to be straight forward. She looked at him with eyes that seemed to look right in Craig's soul and said "The logic tests that I ran, and there were quite a number of them, turned up no error in the logic circuits or the science computer as a whole."

Craig's smile quickly faded into nothingness, and quickly gave rise to a rather dark, grim look. He knew the implications of this news was far reaching and deep rooted. "Thank you, my dear. Thank you for the report." Craig paused a moment to look around the bridge. "Please excuse me now I have some urgent business to attend to."

Matt was briskly walking down the wide corridor to meet his compatriot Valerie in order to walk with her to a meeting. Henry Thompson had called Matt on the intercom a few minutes before saying he had the results of Ted's identity scan. Normally, only one person was to have true knowledge of an amnesia victim's true identity. This was because some years ago it had been found to be a detriment to recovery for an amnesia victim to have true knowledge of who they were. It, usually, just led to frustration and mental blocks. Matt wanted Valerie to have that 'true' knowledge too, since, at the moment, she was working so closely with Ted. Having 'true' knowledge might help her either in defense of or treatment of Ted.

The walk down the corridor was a welcome relief from the constant planning that he'd been doing. It was a very important crisis on Delta Five, probably the biggest of the century, certainly the biggest of his career. His legs became an extension of his tension. Every movement seemed willfully an effort to release tension. Every muscle tightening seemed like a full days work.

Matt, with his extension efforts, began to sweat in the air conditioned halls. He liked this feeling and made his pace more swift in an effort to release even more tension. He succeeded. He noticed he was almost running and slowed his pace slightly.

All of his troubles seemed to be centered in his legs now. He pumped his legs forward as if riding an aero-bike and the motion felt good. He could feel his arteries pumping harder, his veins filling with more and more blood to keep up his pace. He began to sway his arms to and from to make his heart beat ever harder. He was delighted by the fact that the bottoms of his feet were tingling.

By this time he was almost to Medbay anyway so Matt wiped his forehead in a vain attempt to clean himself of the perspiration that had become his friend.

When Matt stepped near the door to Medbay, the glossy gray doors was pulled from his view. Polly Longbow was the first person Matt saw. "Hello captain," came Polly's voice.

With his feet throbbing in relaxation as if resting after a climax of momentous proportions, Matt

said, "Hello. Is Dr. Lomar here? And
can I borrow a towel?"

Polly looked at Matt with bright
eyes and smiled. "Yes to both
questions." Polly happened to have a
towel in her right hand that she threw
to him. Motioning with her left hand
Polly said, "Dr. Lomar is in her
office."

Matt thanked her accordingly,
wiped the sweat from his brow, and
threw the towel in a gray hamper as he
proceeded toward Valerie's office.
Valerie's office door was open. Matt
leaned into the open doorway and said,
"Hey Val, have you got a minute?"

Valerie stopped working with the
medical terminal on her desk and
looked up at Matt. "For you, always.
What is it?"

"Well, it's not really for me. The
results of the identity scan are back,
and I thought you ought to be aware of
who you're dealing with," was Matt's
reply. "Feel like joining me in
conference room 2?"

Valerie almost stumbled on her
words she was so excited, "S-Sure. I'd
like nothing more." She hurriedly
stood up and came out from behind the
desk that had partially concealed her

body. She knew that her medical treatment would be far more potent if she knew the medical history behind whoever Ted was.

CHAPTER 6

In Medbay, Polly was about to start working with Ted, in order for Ted to regain his memory. Through the office door came Matt and Valerie. Polly decided against saying hello, due to their facial expressions being very bland and purposeful. Matt and Valerie were being very cordial as they walked out of Medbay, but there was an air of tension surrounding them.

Turning her attentions toward Ted, who was just waking up, Polly said, "Good day sleepyhead. You sure do have brighter eyes today. How do you feel?"

Ted began rubbing his face and especially his forehead with his open right hand. "My head is splitting," Ted cried out moanfully.

Polly went over to a table layered with an assortment of hypodermics and small bottles filled with liquid. There was also a large portion of pill bottles as well as a few items for covering the skin. Polly started sifting through the pill bottles. Her creamy white arm was cutting through the waves of pills like a hot knife through butter. The arm finally met

its match, then Polly's hand grabbed
the bottle she was after, pulled it
up, and using her other hand opened
the cap. She then grabbed two pills,
and filled a glass of water at the
sink.

Polly then walked up to the right
side of Ted's bed and was reaching for
the U-shaped straw when Ted began to
speak.

"I think I can do without that
straw today."

Polly, knowing she could easily
tell if Ted was having difficulty
swallowing, said, "Sure, we'll give a
try." Polly then put her hand on the
bedrail where the elevation button was
and said, "Now you must tell me if you
feel dizzy or lightheaded in the
slightest?"

"Okay, I promise to tell you," was
Ted's expedient reply.

Polly depressed the button once
again and the head of the bed once
again began to elevate. Polly watched
Ted's eyes intently for any signs of
abnormality. There was none. They were
already past the 45 degrees that was
Ted's stopping point the previous day.
Polly finally stopped the bed at about
75 degrees and said, "I think we'd

better stop here." She put the pills up to Ted's mouth, which was already open, and put the pills and afterward the straw in his mouth.

Ted swallowed without error and afterward said, "Thank you, Polly."

"There that will ease your head," Polly said. she went over to her metal colored station and started pecking at the keys that were on the keyboard. Entering all this data seemed tedious, time consuming, and occasionally not necessary to her, but it was part of the job and she would abide by it.

She began thinking about her time at the medical arts academy back on Janus 6 She had such a lovely time there. Oh, it was a lot of hard work, and it occupied most of her time, but there was something about the freely structured environment that appealed to her. On Janus 6, if you were in class on time, that was great. If you were thirty minutes late, that was cool too. As long as you did the work, and made the grades, they didn't care.

The physical fitness classes were another story. They were rigidly timed and attendance was mandatory. Those were the ones she detested!

In her dreamy state, something brought Ted to mind and she was quickly brought back to the present. Walking over to Ted's bedside she said, "Has that pain reliever stopped your head from hurting?"

Ted was shocked by his own reply, "Yes, it's stopped hurting. I'm amazed that the pain reliever was able to work so fast."

"It pretty strong stuff," Polly said with vigor. "The good thing is, it doesn't have the real bad groggy effect like some pain relievers." Closing with that statement, Polly asked, "Do you feel up to a few mental exercises?"

"What kind of mental exercises?"

"They're called memory assists. They stimulate your brain and help you remember past events," a very assuring Polly replied.

Ted studied Polly's words for a moment, looked at her, and said, "Why not?"

Polly quickly grabbed some round plastic discs that she had gotten from Dr. Lomar and came back to Ted's bedside. Plugging one of the discs into a slot beside the terminal and affixing the terminal so that it

pointed toward Ted, Polly said,
'Concentrate on the images that will
be displayed until your eyes seem to
relax. When that happens, operate this
device to move on to the next frame."
Handing the device to Ted, Polly
activated the terminal.

A brilliantly colored image
appeared on the terminal. It was so
bright that neither Ted nor Polly was
able to resist closing their eyes for
a moment. The image seemed to grow
dimmer, and Ted, opening his eyes and
stared at it intently.

Deciding to move on, Ted clicked
for a new image. Again, he could not
resist closing his eyes, but the
pattern was less brilliant than
before. The pattern he saw this time
was altogether different than the
last.

Even though Ted knew this was
supposed to help he could help but
wonder how long it would take.

It was late afternoon when Matt
and Valerie finally arrived at
conference room two. Henry Thompson
was already in the room waiting very
impatiently. He thought about scolding
the tardy pair, but it would be at a

great risk and he quickly decided against it.

After saying all the niceties of meeting, the stern captain said, "Well, Lieutenant Thompson, what information do you have to share about our visitor?"

An unusually grievous Henry said, "Well sir, I think you're going to find the result of the scan enlightening, but I went ahead and did some background research on my own, and I'm afraid it's not good."

Matt, with strong curiosity and concern for his ship, asked, "What's the bad news?"

"Sir, I'm afraid the identity of our guest is Peter Topper," Replied Henry.

With strong vigor, Valerie exclaimed, "Do you mean the mercenary?"

Henry in a low tone answered, "I'm afraid so, Dr. Lomar, and he's laying unguarded in your Medbay."

Matt broke the conversation up by calling out on the console before him. "Calling Security."

"Security here," a voice rang out from the intercom.

"Post two security guards outside
of Medbay. High priority," Matt
ordered.

CHAPTER 7

It was night aboard the Orion and Craig still hadn't found the captain. He had failed to answer the intercom and Craig had been unable to locate him by exploring the ship. He had checked every place he could think of: Medbay, conference rooms, the bridge, engineering. Yet, there was no sign of him, even talked to people that had visited those places before or possibly going to wherever the captain was. The only other place Craig could think of checking was the captain's quarters. With it being so late at night now, Craig was certain he would be there.

The decks of the ship were very sparsely filled with personnel. It didn't mean that the ship wasn't operating at top efficiency, it just meant that everyone generally stayed at their post at night.

Little work was done between departments during the simulated nighttime that couldn't be handled via computer link. No meeting of the minds was done, no 'think tanks', no public oratories. The principle behind it was do those kinds of

things during the day to keep traffic
on the decks to a minimum at night,
while the principal staff members
were resting.

Craig's brisk pace didn't keep
him from enjoying the pleasant calm
of night. There was a coolness about
the night, even though, by
comparison, the daytime lights gave
off no heat. Craig supposed it was
the brain's artificial reaction from
having been exposed to sunlight for
so many years. It seemed peculiar
though.

Rounding the final corner of his
journey was a blessing to Craig as
his legs were tiring. Craig pressed
the round button beside the doorway
to Matt's quarters to awaken him. He
pressed it again, and again, and
again, and again. Finally, Matt's
voice pierced the semi-harsh sound of
the door call, "Cut that racket out!
I'm coming as quick as I can."

A quiet Craig, waited patiently
outside the door. It wasn't long
before the gray, metallic door slid
open. Craig said without hesitation,
"Sir, we have an urgent matter to
discuss."

"Well, what is it," the sleepy eyed captain said.

Craig answered, "I think you'd rather hear this news in private sir."

Looking disgusted but motioning the science officer inside the door anyway and sealing the door behind him, a concerned Matt asked, "Now, what's so important?"

"I have completed my analysis of the automatically recorded ship's log from Ted's lifepod. The results show that Ted was in the process of delivering a very large shipment to Delta Five. Delta Five, as you well know is the place where the captures are."

"Did the log say what the shipment was," the captain asked of his chief science officer.

"No. There was absolutely no indication," Craig said.

Matt asked, "Then how did the man end up here?"

"His computer guidance went haywire. I've inspected the lifepod and there are pits as well as burn marks, as if the ship was destroyed."

Craig's raised his eyebrows, "Do you understand what I'm suggesting captain?"

Matt, knowing Ted's, alias Peter Topper, history said with deep concern, "Yes, I do, and I can't say I like it." With a slight hesitation, Matt said, "Lieutenant, assemble the department heads in the main conference room at 8:30am tomorrow morning. I will make a ship-wide announcement at 8:15am following which, I will be in that conference room."

"Yes sir," Craig said in a short breath.

"Excellent work, Craig," Matt thought to add. "I greatly appreciate your diligence and thoroughness. It might be that sort of thing that makes this difficult assignment successful."

Craig, feeling pleased with the encouragement, said, "Thank you very much, sir. I try hard."

"It's very evident in your work, Craig."

"Thank you, sir." Craig bid adieu to his captain, went around the ship informing people of the meeting, then

went back to his cabin and got a
short night's rest.

    The morning came all too quickly.
Craig felt as though someone had
thrown stones at him all night. He
slowly peeled the single layer brown
cover from his body and rose from the
bed.
    He started wiping away the matter
that had built up in the corners of
his eyes from his short night's rest,
then began to disrobe. Stripping off
his red striped underpants, which was
the only night clothing he had on,
Craig turned the sonic shower on,
grabbed a washcloth from the lower
bathroom cabinet, and stepped in the
stall.
    Craig had long since gotten used
to sonic showers. He had really
gotten to enjoy them on Armis 6,
where he had his first, and only, pet
iguana. People always thought it was
a strange pe t to have, but he knew
the warmth and affection his pet
could give.
    Gantor would eat from Craig's
hand, something an iguana was
supposed to never do. It wasn't too
hard to make Gantor put away his

shyness about eating. All it took was some gentle coaxing.

The iguana would play with Craig by slapping his long tail up against his body. If he didn't pay attention, the severity of the slapping would increase.

As Craig finished up his shower and dressed, he couldn't help but remember the death of his friend Gantor and he could not help but be saddened. Gantor wrapped himself around an electrical science project that Craig was building; It emitted warmth, which iguanas like. Craig, knowing its instability, spent an hour trying to get Gantor to move off of the project. When he finally moved, one of Gantor's toes hit an exposed circuit and it electrocuted him. Craig was able to force him off the project, but it was too late. Gantor was dead.

Craig held a burial ceremony for his pet. There was him and one other person, Veronica, in the back yard. The ceremony went quickly and Veronica, like most of his friends were compassionate about the whole thing.

The friends on Armis 6 that Craig had were not unlike the friends he had now. Although, there was an officer that reminded him a lot of himself. He was strong willed and wanted, very badly, to be a captain in charge of a ship of his own.

They knew each other since childhood and got along exceedingly well. They had made many pacts, but the one that stood out from the rest was one they had made concerning command. They agreed to never let rank interfere with their friendship. Of course, they realized, much later in life, that rank dictates everything concerning a Space Patrol relationship.

Fortunately, they had never been stationed at the same outpost, or the same ship. They had remained pen pals to this very day. Craig was very happy they had. It provided him with an outlet for his frustrations and emotions.

Having finished getting ready to leave his room, Craig took a few deep breaths to regain his composure and stepped out the door.

The conference room was filled
with people by the time Matt arrived.
There was chattering going on in all
directions as shipboard personnel
related idle stories and ship's
gossip. They seemed unusually
talkative today, but Matt supposed it
was due to the fact that they were to
be in orbit around Delta Five around
midday. Matt quickly quieted them all
down by saying, "Please take your
seats." Everyone quickly stopped
talking and seated themselves at the
nearest chair.

Matt was to reiterate and
elaborate on the very general ship-
wide announcement he had just made
concerning the need to keep Ted in
Medbay as much as possible. He waited
patiently as everyone was being
seated.

When the department heads were
sitting silently in their chairs Matt
began his oration. "Fellow crew
members, late last night news came to
me, by way of science officer Holt,
that could affect our mission. In
accordance with regulations I can
reveal our visitors true identity
under potentially threatening
situations to key personnel, but I

warn you, anyone who reveals this information to others will be dealt with extremely harshly."

Everyone was listening with great curiosity. They had often wondered about their visitor. Especially curious was Commander Frank Doan who had greeted Ted outside his lifepod. Ever since that day, Frank had been kept occupied with a routine maintenance assignment.

Every officer had to go on it in his or her department every now and then. A tour of maintenance duty lasted three months. The time between tours varied by how many people were in the particular department.

Frank's tour of maintenance duty was almost over. By attending the meeting he was trying to catch up on ship's business.

Matt, continuing his speech, said, "I deem you, the heads of departments that will be highly involved in our current assignment, as key personnel. Our visitors name is Peter Topper." There were a few gasps from the room.

"For those of you who are unfamiliar with Mr. Topper, he is a mercenary for hire. The analysis of his computer log indicates he was on course for Delta Five when his navigation computer, evidently, went haywire."

Matt's eyebrows arched a tad to show his concern at this point and then continued his dissemination. "I say evidently because there is the fact that we don't know how Mr. Topper got the injury to his head. There is sufficient reason, in my opinion, to indicate that his whole story may be simply a cover story to get Ted on board our ship."

It may also be possible that he was attacked by some of his enemies and truly does have amnesia. Regardless, Peter Topper is an undeniably clever and dangerous individual who will stop at nothing to complete his mission whatever it may be."

Continuing, Matt said, "Due to the possibility of Peter Topper's possible ruse, I strongly suggest that you and your departments take precautionary measures to insure the crew's well being. I also suggest that his mobility around the ship be limited."

Having said what he wanted, Matt concluded by saying, "Now, if there are no questions, this meeting is over."

Everyone in the room had questions, but no one dared ask them.

CHAPTER 8

It was close to midday on the bridge, the morning had gone by without incident, and the Orion was about to pull into orbit around Delta Five. The ship had been slowing down for numerous hours and the crew was preparing to make contact with the inhabitants of Delta Five, and thereby Joseph Cartier.

Everyone on the bridge, including Craig, was preparing to make contact with Cartier. The only exception seemed to be the captain, who was giving the orders necessary to achieve a standard orbit. With seemingly exacting precision, he gave orders in due succession.

Craig, who had studied the captain's testing manual long and hard over his long tenure with the Crystal Alliance, knew, by heart, the succession of orders that were required. Unfortunately, his desire for a position as the captain of his own ship in the alliance had never been met.

Craig had an unerasable blot on his record. He had been foolish enough to let himself be swayed into a mischievous prank, the theft and hiding of another cadet's dress uniform, right before graduating ceremonies were held. The maligned young man reported the theft and an investigation was launched.

The investigation eventually revealed the entire plot and its perpetrators. The incident went on the permanent records of the three young men, and had forever marred their reputations.

The Alliance held their good values very high and severely frowned on their traitors. Craig had always regretted letting himself be involved with such an incident. He knew he had conned himself into believing it was not his fault, but he also knew that was untrue. He was as much to blame as anyone. With that knowledge came a relentless sick feeling at the pit of Craig's stomach.

He knew that the incident was conduct unbecoming an officer. He had managed to persuade Central Command to give him the position of science officer aboard the Orion, but he thought he would never be able to convince them of his suitability for a captaincy based upon the amount of trouble he had last time.

He had to recover quickly though. The ship had been locked into an orbit around Delta Five, and it was Craig's turn to give sensor information.

"No surprises in the sensor readings. It's just like we expected, pretty calm with the exception of a violent storm at the southern polar region." 'Pretty calm', Craig said it very easily, without thought, but everything was not calm. The whole planet was on edge. "The Aries and the Centari are not here yet, which is surprising considering they were closer than we were."

Matt's voice rang out in all directions from his chair in the center of the bridge, "Let's find out why; Lieutenant O'hara patch me through to Admiral Rutherford."

"Yes sir." After a brief pause Melanie said, "On screen, captain."

"Admiral Rutherford, we're in orbit around Delta Five. Sir, we expected that the Aries and Centari would be here before we arrived. I'd like to know if I should contact them en route to coordinate our efforts?"

"I regret to inform you that the Aries and Centari are dealing with other emergencies that are as vital as the situation at Delta Five. I'm sorry to do this to you Matt, but that's the job you and your crew have drawn."

"I understand. Wish us luck."

"I hope that won't be necessary, but may you and your crew have no troubles. Rutherford out."

A few seconds after the transmission from the admiral, Ms. O'hara, the communications officer, said, "Transmission coming in from the planet, captain."

"Put it on the main viewscreen," Matt said.

The viewscreen in front of the helm and navigation consoles lit up once again. On the screen was the image of Cartier. "Do I have the pleasure of addressing Captain Matt Roberts?"

The attitude and calmness of Cartier was nothing like Matt had expected. "This is Captain Roberts. Mr. Cartier, we seem to have a very precarious situation on our hands. How do you suggest we proceed?"

Cartier paused for a moment, as if he had not thought this far ahead. With a hesitation he said, "I, and a couple of my comrades could come aboard ship for an initial meeting to discuss some issues."

Matt was dissatisfied at the answer Cartier had given. It ruined their plans for the sensor transceiver listening device they had discussed. "That will be fine, Mr. Cartier."

"Please, call me Joe. Everyone else does," said Cartier with a smile on his face.

With a chuckle Matt replied, "All right, Joe. To safeguard you and your party's arrival we'll send one of our shuttles down to meet you."

"That won't be necessary captain. We have several shuttles down here. How about in an hour," Cartier asked.

Matt was glad Cartier said 'in an hour'. That would give him and his staff time to prepare for his arrival, especially him. "That will be fine. I'll see you then. Roberts out," Matt said, and then the viewscreen went blank.

CHAPTER 9

The shuttle bay on the top, left wing of the Orion opened from both sides as the rectangular shaped shuttle approached. The shuttle had tapered edges that represented the light-gray beauty of the slender shuttle exceedingly well. The front of the shuttle had three equal size windows from which the pilots could be seen, the sides had one circular portal, and the rear had two funnel-shaped shields for the engines.

From the shuttle's vantage point the many large weapons on the Orion could be seen. Each gun was equal to the mass of the seemingly minute shuttle. The guns were slender things, but if all of them were to fire at once they could destroy Delta Five. All that would remain would be rubble.

The shuttle slowly maneuvered itself over the minute opening in the Orion, and began to slowly descend onto the landing pad inside the ship. The shuttle's four landing struts cushioned the shuttle's landing with a springy bounce. The shuttle bay quickly pressurized while a reception

committee waited outside the bay
door. The committee consisted of
Matt, Craig, Tactical Commander Ben
Waters, and Frank Doan who had just
got a minor reprieve from the
maintenance assignment.

Frank had finished the
maintenance but technically was still
on the routine maintenance
assignment. Matt wanted him involved
in the negotiations, but naturally he
had to be involved from the very
start. Besides, Frank would have just
been taking care of minor issues for
the rest of his tour anyway.

When the hiss of pressurization
was over, the Orion's committee
stepped out onto the shuttle bay to
greet Cartier and his party. When the
shuttle's doors slid open, Cartier,
another man, and a dark haired woman
stepped out. Matt began to greet
their 'guests', "Welcome aboard the
Orion gentleman and lady. I'm Captain
Matt Roberts. To my right is
Commander Frank Doan, to my left is
our General Science Officer Craig
Holt, to his left is Tactical
Commander Ben Waters."

"Thank you, Captain Roberts. As
you can see I brought some advisors

of my own," as Cartier motioned first to his right, then to his left he continued, "the Pak's chief advisor, General Alonzo Cane, my cohort, Maggie Rem."

"Shall we adjourn ourselves to the Main Conference Room," asked Matt.

Cartier answered with a wry wit, "Well I don't think this shuttle bay would be appropriate for our discussions."

Everyone in the room chuckled slightly. With that said, Matt began leading everyone to the conference room. When they got outside the door, there were three security guards wearing brown helmets and tan uniforms with a star shaped crest on both shoulders.

Matt turned around after the shuttle bay doors closed and began to apologize. "I'm sorry to need to ask your patience, Mister Cartier, but in this type of situation you know that the security guards are mandatory."

"Quite understandable captain," Cartier said, "it's a good policy. In fact, I was the one that suggested it be made a standard, mandatory procedure. Please call me Joe."

"Joe it is," Matt said as he turned back around and began to lead the people down the corridor. The area was cluttered with people. Almost all of them were doing work directly associated with Joe Cartier's onslaught of Delta Five: transporting data, working on invasion plans and protocols, assessing strengths and weaknesses, etc.

Joe Cartier was truly amazed at the ship. He was looking at everything. He had been in charge of, indirectly, administrating these fine vessels, but he had never been aboard one. How truly outstanding it was. And the Orion was one of newest in the fleet so her equipment was truly modern. Computer terminals were everywhere and all of them lit up with assorted data. He had been aboard shuttles and luxury liners all of his life since he was born into a rich family, but nothing quite like this.

In the corridor, Cartier noticed a dark haired man clothed in a drab medical gown, and blue pants. The man walked upright, but without purpose. Aha! Joe Cartier had found one of

things he had been looking for. It
was so right that he almost could not
contain the smile that tore at the
corners of his mouth. He had not
expected to find it so early in the
journey through the ship, but there
it was.

When the party of people entered
the conference room, Matt took a seat
at his usual spot beside the control
panel built in to the table.
Immediately afterward, without
invitation, the rest of the
negotiators took their seats.

The somewhat wrinkled captain was
the first to speak. "Where shall we
begin Joe?"

Joe Cartier responded with a
surprise, "Your party shall not be
negotiating. Instead, we prefer a
neutral negotiator."

Shocked by Cartier's statement,
Matt raised his voice to say, "What?
Tell me I didn't hear you right?"

"We prefer a neutral negotiator,"
Maggie Rem said.

"Well, I wish we would had known
so we could have prepared better.
It'll be a few days until we can
transport a skilled negotiator in
here."

Cartier said, "We mean a 'neutral' negotiator."

"What do you mean," Matt said.

"Surely you can't mean someone with no negotiating experience," an astounded Matt asked.

"Yes, that's exactly what we mean," Cartier said.

"That is a highly unusual request Joe. I am prepared to accept your terms, however, on one condition, we pick the negotiator from our crew," Matt said.

"That won't be acceptable captain. We would like to pick our own negotiator," the general said.

"Those are terms we can't abide by," Matt indicated.

"Then we will be forced to round up some of the Alphorzia and destroy it. Afterwards we'll shut down the mining robots and shut down all the shipping to and from Delta Five. I have men stationed all around the plant. I don't want to hurt anybody, but..."

Matt stopped him by saying, "All right, all right, we get the idea. May we at least select a person to go with this negotiator?"

"No. That will not be acceptable," the general quickly said.

Matt replied, "All right, may we at least have a moment to discuss the issue."

Cartier smiled and said, "That won't be necessary captain. We saw the person we'd like to negotiate with on the way here."

"Who is he? What is his name," Matt asked.

Cartier, perplexed, replied, "Well, I don't know his name, but he had black hair, blue pants, and wore a medical gown. Do you have any idea of who that could be?"

Matt paused a moment, then said, "Craig, flash up the holographic image of every patient in the medical sections." After a slight pause, he added, "Be sure to sort them."

Craig, knowing exactly what the captain was referring to, stood up and started working with the control panel in front of the captain. In a few moments he said, "I've programmed the projector to rotate the images clockwise, pause, then move on. If you recognize the person you're referring to, tell me, and I can

freeze the image." Craig then pushed
a button to start the display.
"Please be patient. There are 57
patients currently residing in these
medical stations."

One by one the images of patients
appeared in full holographic detail.
It wasn't the first one, or the
second, or the 29th, or the 45th. In
fact, it was the very last record
they viewed.

"That's him," Cartier shouted.

Matt quickly said, "I'm sorry.
That's Ted, or so we've been calling
him. He's not part of our crew.
Besides, he's got amnesia. He won't
do. Pick anyone else."

"No sir, that's our man. The fact
that he's not part of the crew makes
it better. The amnesia make it even
better. It's non-negotiable," Cartier
threatened.

'How in the name of hell did this
madman see Ted,' Craig wondered.

CHAPTER 10

"Do you have any other questions, Ted," asked Frank.

"Yes, I'm not sure I'm clear on how I'm supposed to negotiate from the standpoint of individual issues when there is only one issue they're interested in?"

"That's not quite true," Frank said. Being certain to choose his words carefully, he continued, "Find out what their grievances are and negotiate a settlement on each, one at a time."

From his usual chair in the conference room, Matt broke in saying, "Yes, Ted. They've obviously got disagreements with the controlling party of Omega III. Find out what those differences are, then resolve them. If we can make compromises between the Pak's desires and the ruling government of Omega III, maybe we can resolve the situation through peaceable means." The captain started to stare intently at Ted to add power to his next words. "Regardless, the high council will not, under any terms, give them any kind of legal immunity from these acts. Don't volunteer that information. Of course, Cartier probably knows that though."

"Okay, Captain Roberts. I think I understand now."

"Any other questions," Frank asked.

"Will I still be able to continue my working towards getting my memory back?"

Matt quickly answered, "No, I'm afraid that's been suspended for the time being."

"May I ask why? I mean I'm really anxious to put this behind me."

"We just feel that negotiating with a band of, what are now criminals, will be hard enough," said Matt knowing what a recollection of Ted's past, at the wrong moment, could do. If Ted were to mistakenly say a wrong word or two, everything could be lost.

"How much time will I spend negotiating?"

Frank reluctantly answered, "Well, Ted, I guess that all depends on a number of things."

"How much time is about average," said a frustrated Ted.

Matt answered in the only way available to him, "How much time is not important. It is the difficulty of the negotiations that is the important thing here."

Ted backed off slightly, "And how difficult is negotiating?"

"Sometimes very."

"All right, I see your point," said Ted.

Jane Reaton was busy reprogramming the engineering computer core when Craig arrived. A junior grade engineer had discovered a flaw in one of the dynamic subroutines that prevented the automatic water cut off valves for the showers from operating.

The large main room was filled with people sitting or standing at computer terminals. The computer's room was sealed off from the rest of the ship by a transparent wall. There were several people in the room working the massive digital storage units, keeping them up to date with system corrections and additions. Jane was busily consulting with one of the other technicians.

Craig waited for a drop in conversation before he greeted her. When the time was right he said, "Hi, Jane."

"Hi, slugger," said Jane feeling rather chipper. "How's the light of my life doing today?"

"I'm great. What put you in such a good mood?"

"I'm not sure. I just woke up feeling good about everything."

"Well I'm certainly glad of that. It's not too often you get like this. How about a few hours of fun tonight at my cabin?"

"Sounds great to me. Is 7 O'clock okay dear," asked Jane with a sly grin.

"That will be splendid." Changing the subject Craig said, "Meanwhile, I was wondering if you could help me with an investigation I'm conducting?"

"Sure. Is it ship's business or what," Jane asked curiously.

Craig motioned Jane inside her vacant office. Once inside he spoke to her in a hushed voice. "It concerns an odd situation aboard the ship, but I have no clearance to investigate this matter. Jane, I'm asking you very kindly to keep this matter silent. I could into a lot of trouble if my investigation came to light."

"Of course I will. As long as it doesn't hurt anyone."

"There was an incident about a few hours ago. Cartier and his party came aboard and they saw Ted, our visitor. I'm researching how Ted got out of Medbay at such a critical time."

Valerie knew that what was being said was very important and would need the tightest of security. "Yes, I can well see why you would investigate the issue and the need for this investigation to remain covert." Jane closed her remarks by saying, "You can count on me."

Craig felt very good about her response. He knew Jane well enough to know that by the sound of her determined and trusting voice, he could be sure of Jane's silence.

He continued the conversation by saying, "Can we check the medical computer to see why he was out of Medbay?"

As she went to the computer terminal on her desk, Jane said,

"Well, we can check if he was scheduled for any medical tests?" Punching away at the computer for a moment with her slim fingers and semi-long fingernails was an all too familiar experience for her. Suddenly, one of her nails brushed against one of the keys in row above the one she pressing. The pressure made the nail crack. "Dang it, I just can't keep a nail," she said as she finished tearing the nail off with her mouth.

Matt tried to console her. "Don't worry dear. I love you anyway."

Jane pressed the enter key and the computer began to retrieve the data that the lovely lady had requested. Once she read the lettering that appeared up on the screen, Jane said, "No. No tests were scheduled for him on that day."

She thought she could have guessed the results of that search. Whoever was guilty of tampering with crucial schedules like Ted's (at this point anyway) would not be hanging around for their funeral.

The pair tried several more queries to the computer, all with as much success as the first. In the meantime, there had been several knocks at the door from people asking job related questions and important news. Neither of them seemed to very bothered by the intrusions. But, the knocks became more numerous.

Finally, Jane said, "Craig, we've been at this quite a while with no success. Evidently the information you're seeking is going to take a long while to find. Why don't ..."

Craig had already figured what she was going to say and could tell her duties were very pressing. "Why don't I let you get on with your job and get back to me later. After all, this is extracurricular."

Jane's face twisted into a look that said, 'I don't want to hurt you, but I must be elsewhere.' Her cheeks were raised high and her shoulders were elevated slight, "Do you mind terribly?"

Craig was very compassionate. "Not at all, my dear. You can tell me what you find out tonight."

"Thank you. I shall not forget about this. I'm sorry, we're having to overhaul some circuits today. I won't forget about this matter though."

Craig said, "All right, honey," then left.

In the same shuttle bay as the Cartier and his party entered from, Matt, Ted, Frank Doan, and several shuttle pilots stood arguing.

"You just can't do this, captain," a very stressed Frank said.

"I'm captain of this tub and I say I can, Frank."

"It would expose you to too much danger. We can't afford to lose you, especially not at this time," Frank said.

"I know about the dangers, but I feel by my transporting Ted to the conferences on the planet, I'll be able to gain more insight into the situation than a junior officer would," said a determined Matt.

"You're right, of course, but the danger is too great," Frank reiterated. "Captain you are the most vital crew member aboard and we can't afford any injury to you, or for you to be captured."

Matt felt frustrated by the argument. He decided to put an end to it one way or the other. "You and everyone aboard this ship needs for

me to make effective decisions
concerning this crisis. I don't think
I can do that by staying aboard this
ship. I need to survey the site,
myself, to have the data I need to
make the most effective decisions
concerning the lives aboard this
ship. Like it or not, I have to go."

Frank reluctantly admitted defeat
on the issue. The captain had let him
know, politely, that he felt he
needed to go and was not going to
take 'no' for an answer. Frank
resigned his position by saying,
"Okay, captain. I realize that we all
need to do some things that aren't
very popular to do our job. I wish
you and Ted luck on your trip."

"Thank you, Frank," Matt said
gratefully.
He would need good luck if he was to
be successful at his secret mission.

Ted and Matt walked toward the
open door of the oblong shuttle. The
shuttle was subtly different from the
one that Cartier and his party came
in. The top and bottom corners were
more subtly tapered. The front of the
shuttle had the same type of windows
for the pilots, but the windows were
larger due to there being more of an

angle toward the front of the shuttle.

Matt sat in the pilot seat and Ted, following Matt's lead, seated himself in the co-pilots seat. While Matt checked all the controls to see if they were in proper working order, Ted became more familiar with his chair by moving his buttocks around in it.

After he had gotten into a position on the soft seat that seemed comfortable to him, Ted surveyed the massive control panel before him. He thought he must have mastered all these controls at one time in his life, but it seemed beyond him as to how.

Suddenly, Matt's voice broke, piercing his thoughts. "Preparing for takeoff." Matt pressed a button on the panel that closed and locked the once open door they had walked through.

"We hear you, captain. Tell us when you're ready for us to open the bay doors," a crisp voice over the loudspeaker in the shuttle said.

"We're ready. I've done my pre-flight check already and sealed the shuttle door," Matt said.

"Hold on. We're clearing out the ground crew now."

A few moments passed by as Matt became increasingly aggravated at the lack of efficiency of the shuttle bay crew. 'Oh well. That wouldn't be his responsibility much longer,' he thought.

"We're depressurizing the bay now captain," Frank Doan said. "Depressurization complete. Now opening the bay doors. You can begin your ascent now."

"See you people later," Matt said into the microphone built onto the headset he was wearing. Matt could feel the shuttle lift up off the deck of the ship. He carefully guided the shuttle straight up towards the now wide open door above it. He went very slow so if there was any sudden pull from the ship's artificial gravity, he could easily compensate.

He could see the edge of the bay opening, gently growing nearer and as he past the edge of it, the vastness of space overwhelmed him. Although Matt had been piloting shuttles for over twenty years, this was a point that never failed to put him in utter awe.

When the shuttle was, roughly, five yards from the Orion, Matt turned off the maneuvering thrusters and engaged the main engines. The shuttle was propelled, through Matt's expert guidance, toward the planet. The green oceans of Delta Five gave the planet a light-green hue which Matt found attractive. The water had a few trace elements that gave it the hue, but there was nothing dangerous about it. It had been studied numerous times, but no evidence of ill-effects had ever been proven.

As they neared the landing site that Cartier had transmitted the coordinates to, they saw themselves headed straight for the capitol building. It was a huge complex with a slender tower built of gray stones at the center. The complex snaked out into all directions from the center. The tower was circular with very few windows.

As the shuttle grew ever nearer to the outskirts of the complex, shuttle landing pads could be seen. Matt maneuvered the shuttle over one of the empty pads and began the descent. The gravity on Delta Five was a tad stronger than he expected, but he quickly compensated.

Once they were down, Matt opened the shuttle door. The two men unstrapped themselves and walked out of the shuttle. Two men, one tall and blonde, the other dark haired with a heavy build, came up to them.

The blonde asked, "Which of you is Ted?"

"He is," Matt said, pointing to Ted with his fingers closed and thumb pointing towards Ted.

"Ted, come with me please," the blonde asked in a harsh tone. It was more like a command than a request.

After the two men had left, Matt said to the big man as handed him a disc, "Watch out, you may have a spy among you."

CHAPTER 11

It was a very tense atmosphere in the main conference room as Ben Waters, Frank Doan, and Craig Holt were viewing and listening to the transmissions from the device they had hid on Ted's left arm. The device was extremely small and sensitive. They had stealthily hid it on Ted while he was asleep from a gas that they had introduced into his room the previous night.

They were viewing a long corridor with many doors, lavishly decorated with gold paint, and a few interconnecting hallways on the wall viewscreen. Now and then another figure would be walking in one of the adjoining hallways, or coming out of one of the doors in the main corridor, but such events were infrequent.

Not surprisingly, there was very little conversation as the figures walked down the corridor. From the passers by, there was no conversation, almost as if they knew they were being observed.

Ben looked down at the equipment that was by his side. Having viewed

the recordings that the utensils were
making he decided to cut the profane
silence in the conference room. "So
far we're getting a getting a good
sketch of the building. It doesn't
seem to be any different than the
original blueprints."

Turning his head toward Ben,
Craig said, "That's good. Let's hope
it keeps going that way," Turning his
head back toward the viewscreen Craig
noticed the two people were turning
into one of the adjoining hallways.

"I guess the captures are not
stationed at the center tower," Ben
said.

The viewscreen started to show
interference. The picture was getting
filled with white blotches and there
was some distortion. The buildup was
slow, but eventually the entire
picture, sensor net, and audio were
completely blocked.

The three men waited for the
interference to pass, figuring that
there was a metal conduit that was
blocking the transmission. They were
correct. The interference slowly
subsided, but it was followed by
another wave of interference as
assumingly another conduit passed. It

subsided once more. There was another surge of interference, but this time the picture did not come back.

All three of the men stared at the solid white speckled screen for a considerably long time. None of them wanted to admit their efforts had failed to work the first time at bat. They didn't want to admit they had lost the battle. Most of all though, they didn't want this loss to pull down their self esteem.

"What happened," exclaimed Frank, questioning the reasonableness of a long blackout.

"I don't really know," Craig said. "I guess it could be a solid metal roof, but we all know that there are supposed to be no roofs of that type in the building." Craig looked rather solemn. He hoped that Frank had an answer. Unfortunately, he did not.

"I don't know either," Frank said. "Jot the time down Craig. At least we'll have that information. I suggest we hang around here a while to see if anything further develops."

"Well, I think maybe it was by design that we lose track of them. The man we're dealing with is not a fool. What bothers me is they were able to disrupt our transceiver so quickly," said Craig with a stretched face as if in disbelief.

Ben said, "Yes. I mean we're talking about a sophisticated device that cannot be easily jammed. It can be disrupted very easily, but not jammed."

"Jammed, disrupted. It's all the same thing to me," Frank said.

"But it's not all the same," Ben sharply pointed out. "With disruption, the signal will most likely be partially blocked. With jamming, the signal will be totally blocked. We've previously concluded that there are no real totally 'dead' spots for the signal in the original blueprints. Isn't it possible..."

Frank interrupted Ben's speech. He knew of Ben's suspicious nature and wanted to avoid Ben, and others, from forming opinions from a loosely associative theory which had no conclusive evidence behind it. "Ben, you said the key words yourself, 'in the original blueprints.' Don't forget, the blueprints we have are 12 years old. That whole building could have been renovated for all we know. Let's not jump to conclusions."

"Craig," Ben said, "What do you think?"

"I don't know. But, I refuse to go off angry and try to pin my suspicions about something that easily be explained on somebody or something," Craig said. "Let's not forget, we have very little concrete information. I refuse to even speculate about a cause until we get more information."

Ben appeared miffed. "I guess you're right."

When the meeting adjourned, Ben hurried to the computer center. Anxious to try his notion of using the existing satellites to map the layout of the capitol building.

When he arrived, the many rows of computer terminals were, although they were long, virtually filled. While he was surveying the surroundings, Ben spotted a gray terminal midway back on the second row and hurried to it for fear that he might have to wait if someone else beat him to it. Luckily, he was able to obtain the seat. He knew that everyone else was working on the same project as him, but he was extremely anxious to see the current layout of the building. Almost all other things depended on knowing the exact layout of the building.

He passed the main screen quickly, punching in his identification name and password. His first task was to establish a link between the communications computer and engineering computer. This was no easy task for anyone, not even him. Getting two computers to talk to each other was very hard and usually required special computer hardware.

Luckily, the computer personnel had been, and still were, adding publicly available subroutines to the library of files, stored on the central computer, for this purpose. A person that needed a particular subroutine for his particular interconnecting program could simply copy a subroutine from that public library into his own program to make his work much easier.

The subroutine that he copied would serve as a useful tool to connect the two, or more, computers. Eventually, a person would only have

to write four or five instruction
lines into a program. The rest would
be from these mini-programs.

Unfortunately, they were not
through writing these mini-programs,
so he would have to write a large
portion of the program himself.

The next several hours for Ben
were filled with a lot of a lot of
sweaty moments and a few moments with
his head in his hands. Problem after
problem came up, but Ben was able to
solve most of them fairly quickly.

His tension could be easily
noticed by the rigid outline of neck
muscles. His eyes were totally
focused on the screen in front of
him. As they glanced back and forth
and darted to different places on the
screen one could easily tell, 'this
man was not only doing his job, but
he was on a personal mission as
well.'

Ben knew that his goal was not
only in pursuit of truth but also for
him to be hailed as a Hero of the
truth. He wanted to bask in the
applause of all who know or knew him.
To do that he knew he would have to
do something outstanding, something

not necessarily gallant, but something no one else had done. He knew that it had to reveal a major shameful plot.

When he was finished with his program, Ben pressed against the floor with his legs to tip his chair onto its rear legs and breathed a sigh indicative of a job well done.

His job was not, however. Now it was time for the real test, to see if the satellites, in orbit about the planet, could penetrate the complex's walls. Ben managed a smile in early anticipation of the results of his scan as he slowly pressed the button that would start his program.

There was a single flashing word on Ben's screen: 'IN PROGRESS'. He had not programmed all the niceties of many other programs; he was far too anxious for that. The dim white letters seemed to say, 'I'm going to work.'

But, it was not to be; there was an error in the program.

Error 47
Invalid Match in line 31

"Error 47," Ben mumbled to himself in both anger and disappointment as he began to look at his program. 'The error says, something is not defined right,' he thought angrily. He looked up at his variable definitions and spotted the error after a lot of studying. "Ah, there you are you," he said feeling pleased with himself. He then corrected the error and ran the program again.

Error 17
Missing ")" in line 48

He began looking at his program once more. This time he corrected the error easily. Once more he tried to run the program.

This time the program ran without errors. His screen first filled with an external sketch of the complex, then layer by layer the screen totally filled the building with white space as solid as brick wall.

"Damn it," he accidentally said aloud. It wasn't working; it wasn't showing any scrap of detail.

On the bridge, Frank Doan was babysitting all the routine, crisis preventing, functions of the ship. The bridge was where he and the staff could monitor every aspect of the ship's functions, the planet, and space in general. The long range scanners could even monitor a small distance beyond the realm of the current solar system.

He was currently personally monitoring the planet using the science station. As he peered at the digital display in the center of the sloped counter top before him, he thought to himself, "Boy, do I need a break." He had worked hard all day and considered going straight to bed after his shift was over.

The younger you are when going into the academy, the less time they train you. It was thought that the younger brains could absorb information quicker. Frank thought that he must have been an exception. He was never very quick to learn things in school, and he always had to study harder than most of his friends.

After he got through the academy, by sheer luck he thought, he spent a lot of time studying his old textbooks. After he started applying what he had that he never really learned, he was delightfully surprised to find that he knew a lot more than he thought he did.

"Engineering calling the bridge," came Scott Talby's voice on the intercom.

"Bridge here, Commander Doan speaking," Frank replied after he pushed a small white button on the panel beside the display.

"You asked for a status report. There's some plasma buildup inside the engine walls, but as soon as we discharge it, it won't be problem. Nothing else to report," Scott Talby said.

"Good Scott. Keep up the good work. Frank out."

Frank's attention went back to the display before him. While he was busily pushing touch sensitive buttons to get a more accurate reading another voice spoke to him.

"Commander Doan, I have a suspicious long range sensor reading that I think you ought to take a look at," said Mr. Kyan.

Frank rose up from his chair hurriedly as he said, "Put it on the viewscreen lieutenant."

The viewscreen changed from a large, clear, picture of the planet surface to one of a small, distant planet that almost could not be seen. Frank said, "Give me full magnification Mr. Rupart."

"Full mag," Pete said as he touched a button. The planet became larger, but not much. It was large enough now though to see a ship peeking its head out from the edges of the dark figure.

"Can anyone here tell what kind of ship that is?"

The room was filled with silence, apparently no one could. For a moment, any noise would have been shattering. "Ms. O'hara try and contact that ship," Frank ordered.

Melanie continued with her console as she responded, "I've been trying sir and there is no reply to my hail."

Frank said, "Mr. Kyan, round me up two pilots with combat experience. I want to know exactly what's out there and the captain is going to want to know too."

CHAPTER 12

The shuttle slowly lifted off the pad a few minutes after Matt followed Ted into the shuttle. Matt had considered the session fairly long for negotiations to take, but he wasn't really concerned about it. There was a lot to discuss between the two sides.

After the meeting, during the meal that Cartier had invited them to, neither Cartier nor Ted had few words to say directed in Matt's direction. It was just the general dinner chat. Matt thought there would have been some discussion on their progress or some issue briefing at a minimum, but there was no mention of issues period, just idle talk about how it was going. They all agreed it was a good getting acquainted with the issues meeting, but Matt felt like something remained unsaid.

As the shuttle penetrated the rim of the atmosphere Matt asked of Ted, who was in the co-pilot's seat, "I bet the negotiations were very tense."

All he got in return for his effort from Ted, who sat loosely in his chair with his face now pointed in Matt's direction, was, "Not really."

Matt wished Ted had given him more information, but it was no big deal. Besides, they were going into the shuttle bay now. When the ship landed and the area was pressurized again, Matt and Ted stepped out of the shuttle and were greeted by Craig and the bay crew.

Matt and Ted walked out of the shuttle looking tired. Piloting a shuttle was not that easy. Other shuttles had self guidance, autopilots, and all the modern conveniences, but it was thought that the Space Patrol had enough conveniences. The shuttles were constructed last and there was a major budget crunch at the time, so the shuttles were redesigned at the last minute to be economical to build.

The time on the planet was not hectic at all for Matt. During the meeting he was just escorted to a waiting area and entertained himself with the paraphernalia that was at hand, after all, he had to keep up appearances. Afterwards, they had had the dinner of course.

"Hello captain," said Craig as the ground crew started to take care of the shuttle. "How did everything go?"

"Fine, fine, it was a good getting acquainted meeting so they tell me. How did everything go while I was gone," Matt responded.

Craig replied, "No problems on this end."

"Great! If you would escort Ted to his quarters, I'd like to go to my cabin and get some shuteye," Matt said.

"Aye, Aye, skipper," Craig replied already trying to lead Ted with a wave of his right hand. He continued motioning towards Ted until Ted started walking in the direction of the far door to the shuttle bay.

Once outside the door, the duo made a right turn and began walking down the corridor. Craig was still thinking about how the man next to him, Ted, alias Peter Topper, got out of his cabin during the time Cartier came aboard. Things that he wasn't sure about always bothered him. He had always been a curious person.

Anything that he didn't have full
knowledge, that he felt it useful to
know, always had bothered him.

Some fool had deliberately or
accidentally disobeyed orders. It was
the deliberate part that he was most
concerned with. The authority to
control Ted's whereabouts at that
time, must have come from a senior
officer, namely one of the department
heads.

Everybody was to have understood,
from the captain and the department
heads, that Ted was not to have been
out of his cabin during the time that
Cartier was onboard. Disobeying
orders was bad, what was worse is
sabotage. It showed a total disregard
for the safety of the entire ship and
a total disregard for the very
principles of the Space Patrol. It
was the worst thing an officer could
do and that scared Craig.

"Well Mr. Holt, looks like this
is my stop," came Ted's voice from
the breast of his doorway.

Craig had gotten in so much of a
daze about the inconsistencies of his
dilemma that he hadn't noticed they
were nearing Ted's cabin. He took a

step or two further before it dawned
on him that Ted had even spoke. He
looked over his right shoulder and
began to turn around to face Ted
saying, "Oh, I'm sorry. My mind was
just occupied. Of course Ted, have a
great rest."

Ted yawned and retreated into his
cabin with his arms stretched over
his head, as if in sleep.

Craig continued his walk down the
corridor toward the computer center
and Jane. She was probably busy, but
he could always work alone.

A few minutes after Craig had
left, Ted peeked out of his doorway.
Seeing that Craig had vanished from
sight, Ted went down that hall, and
up a deck to Medbay to see Polly.

Polly was busily stirring around
handling various equipment. She was
so busy, she didn't see one of her
favorite patients of the last decade
come in. Ted tried carefully not to
frighten her, but he had to move with
stealth or else Dr. Lomar would see
him. "Polly," he whispered loudly.
"Polly," he whispered again.

This time she noticed him
crouched behind a portable table.

Walking toward his direction she said, "Why are you hiding behind that table?"

"Is doctor Lomar here," whispered Ted.

"No, she's at the lab running some tests. She won't be back for a long time, unless we need her," Polly responded.

Ted stood up. "Good, I'd like to avoid her."

"Why," asked Polly.

Ted, with a shrug of his shoulders said, "I'd just like to that's all. How's life?"

Polly, looking chipper as always, said, "Pretty good actually and how are you?"

"Fair. Let's go in this office a minute and talk," Ted said. With that said, Ted escorted Polly into Dr. Lomar's office and Ted shut the door behind them.

"Polly, this loss of memory is driving me absolutely crazy. Will you help me to get my memory back," said Ted.

Polly threw up her hand flatly pointing up, backed up a step, and said, "Hold it right there. I've got orders not to help you in that area."

"Polly, help me please. This is driving me nuts! Won't you help?"

"No."

"If the circumstances were turned around I'd help you. They suspended it when this conferencing came about," said Ted.

"What reasoning did they give you? They didn't give us any reason," Polly said.

Ted said bluntly, "They just told me that negotiating was too tiring of a job to be combined with my memory work."

Polly smirked a little bit, smiled, and said, "That's sounds like a lame excuse to me." She paused a moment.

Ted broke in on her thoughts by saying, "Isn't there anything you can do?"

"Yes. Wait outside while I call a counselor I know in the Psychiatric Department," Polly said.

"Thank you very much," Ted said.

"Don't thank me yet. I still may not help," Polly said.

Ted said with a smile, "At least you're doing something and I appreciate that." With his gratitude conveyed, Ted turned his attention back to Polly and headed toward the main compartment of Medbay.

Once there he stood patiently with his back to the room he exited. He did not want to watch Polly's movements through the glass for fear he would only build up his hopes, only to have them dashed. That would have been more than he thought he could withstand.

His anticipation grew ever stronger anyway though. He could feel it filling every inch of his body with eager tension. It filled his chest, like a disease moving ever faster through his body, spreading into his arms, legs, hands, feet, and finally his neck and head. The infection grew stronger by the moment as he fought to keep his sanity.

Ted wasn't aware of anything at the moment except his anxiety. Out of sheer torment, he crouched over, balled up his hands, and began swinging his arms toward his legs. His legs did not feel the impacts of his fists, just the tenseness of his body. He didn't really know why he was hitting himself, and he thought it peculiar to say the least, but he could not stop himself.

Pounding ever vigorously with his back toward the object of his tension, Ted's mind was totally oblivious to everything except the door behind him; it was off Cartier, negotiating, the captain, everything… The stress was almost more than he could bear.

Ted stopped pounding when he heard the door behind him open. He quickly straightened up from his crouched position so he would not be thought abnormal.

"Come in please, Ted," Polly told him.

Ted hurried into the office, overly anxious to hear what Polly had to say.

Polly looked at Ted with caring eyes and said, "Well, my friend says that they gave her no explanation as to why you couldn't continue with your memory facilitation exercises. She didn't see where it would hurt, unless you physically couldn't keep up with both memory facilitation and negotiating, but she left it up to me."

Ted began pleading with her. "Oh, please help me?" There was a pitiful

quality to his voice that he hoped
would convey to her his longing for
treatment.

"Don't worry. I've already
decided I'll help you, but only if
you promise me that if it turns out
to be too tiring, you'll stop until
the negotiations are over?
Negotiations come first."

Ted quickly said, "Oh, I promise
you, lovely one. If it's too much
I'll quickly say so."

"All right," Polly said, "Since
Dr. Lomar is out for several more
hours, I'm going to give you a brief
treatment in an isolation chamber,
but since it would look suspicious
for you to be coming back here, I'm
going to give you a portable memory
facilitator."

Ted reached out, with both arms
stretched wide, to hug Polly's neck.
She did not want to allow it at
first, but hesitated slight from her
withdrawal. By the time she regained
her senses, it was too late. Ted
already had her wrapped her up.
Admitting defeat, she stretched her
arms around his upper torso in
return.

They embraced for a few minutes
with Ted whispering thank you to her
every step of the way. The embrace
seemed to last a long time to them
both, but slowly gave way to reality.

Their silence, immediately after
the embrace slowly broke up, but was
indicative of how crucially important
to Ted this was. It was almost as if
his very life depended on it.

Polly was the first one to break
the tension, "I guess you're ready
for your treatment then?"

"You bet," Ted said.

Pointing towards a door in the
rear of Medbay, Polly said, "That's
the door to the isolation room. Enter
7 1 6 D, as in data, the code for
today, and let yourself in. I'll get
the portable memory facilitator and
meet you there in a minute."

"Okay," Ted said.

Polly watched Ted for a second or
two heading for the door she had
pointed out, then exited the office
and headed toward the exit door to
Medbay.

Polly went down the corridor a
short ways, then turned into the
psychiatric department of the ship.
She went straight to their equipment

closet and sifted through a bunch of
devices. Most of them she was
unfamiliar with, but some them she
had had training on in the academy.

 After sifting through quite a
few, she found what she was looking
for at the very back of the closet.
She grabbed it tightly with her right
hand and quickly trailed out of the
department, back down the corridor,
and into Medbay.

 She walked at the same quick pace
to the to door which she had directed
Ted, entered 7-1-6-D on the keypad,
and opened the door.

 "Greetings, oh favorite one,"
said Ted sitting in front of a table,
raising of his left hand.

 Polly replied with a smile, "All
right slicker, you've said your
thanks."

 Ted said, "Yeah, but no thanks is
too much."

 "Well, you can lay off now. I
know you're thankful," Polly said.
With a slight pause she continued,
"This is the portable unit I was
telling you about," she said raising
it up with her arm. She laid it on
the table, undid the heat sensitive
locks, and opened it up.

The inside was simple looking with only a 5" x 5" digital display, four pressure buttons and a much smaller level indicator.

Polly began explaining. "It's quite simple really. The two right buttons that are beside the display at the top, are turn the machine on and off. The bottom two buttons below the indicator, are for the force setting adjustment. You were at level four when they stopped your treatments."

"One question," said Ted, "how do I know when to go up or down a setting?"

"Just time," Polly responded, "The brain has an incredible ability to adapt, and if you keep going up a setting every time you feel like you're getting used to the patterns and intensity of a setting, you almost can't go wrong. If you feel like your mind is in a strain from a setting, then go down a level. The yardstick we use is every seven days go up a level."

"Okay Polly," Ted said.

"Now let's get you set up for a quick treatment before you leave," said Polly.

CHAPTER 13

When Matt walked onto the bridge the next morning he was immediately confronted by his second in command, Frank Doan.

"Captain, sir," Frank said, "we've looked for you for over three hours. I've a reconnaissance group of fighters on their way to Delta 12, the outermost planet in this system, because of a unknown ship that refuses to identify itself."

Matt responded almost humorously, "You could have just looked in my cabin, Frank."

Frank looked stunned. His mouth dropped slightly and his jaws looked limp. His eyes, visibly calculating what to say, couldn't find the right words to fit his stupidity. "I … I … Well, sir, I just didn't think you would be in your cabin at this time of the day."

Matt, of course, realizing Frank had learned his lesson, said, "Don't worry about it. Just try to explore all avenues next time, no matter how ridiculous." Trying not to make the issue look too prominent, Matt said,

"Now what's this you were saying about an unknown ship?"

Frank breathed a sigh of relief at being left off with just a warning. The captain was usually was a stickler about foolish, sloppy, errors, and Frank was lucky enough to only get a warning. "It's just like I said, we've got an unknown ship out there that refuses to answer a hail."

"Did you consider the chance that it might be a derelict?"

"Yes sir, but before we discount it, I want a full report from a scouting party," Frank said.

"I quite agree. How close is the scouting party,"' asked Matt.

Frank said, "About two minutes away. They ought to be able to at least see the vessel pretty good by now."

"Lieutenant O'hara, patch me through to the leader of the scouting patrol," said Matt.

"Yes sir," Melanie said. She fiddled with her controls a moment then said, "Ensign Dar on the speaker sir."

"Ensign Dar, what's it look like out there," Matt asked.

"It appears to be an ore freighter sir," came the ensign's voice.

Matt responded, "Can you patch us into your wing camera, so that we can see it?"

"Yes sir, hold on a moment and I'll tie you in."

After a few moments, The main viewscreen lit up with a view of a fairly recently made freighter. It was pointed in front, then flared out from the tip all the way back behind the planet. The top and bottom of the ship didn't intersect completely at any place except the tip. Everywhere else had an intervening seemingly jagged edged separator.

As the regiment of fighters approached the rear of the ship became visible. On the top of the ship was a diamond shaped raised platform with a rectangular outcropping that was meant for the bridge apparently.

Matt voice broke through the silence. "Ensign, do you see any lights anywhere, or anything to indicate that this vessel is being used?"

"Negative sir," the young man said.

"Check the orbital status of this thing, ensign," Matt ordered.

"Yes sir," the ensign said stopped speaking a moment so he could fiddle with some his cockpit equipment. "Aye sir, it is decaying."

"Ensign is there any chance that this vessel could be storing something, like say, a fighter or a bomb," came Frank's voice.

"Sensor sweeps of the cargo hold are negative, but a bomb is always possible. As far as a bomb, we can't really scan for that sir, but I guess we could monitor the ship," Ensign Dar said.

Matt spoke in finality, "Well, unless my second in command has anything further to check or say, we'll consider this ship a dead issue?"

Frank told the pilot, "Are there any definitive markings such as a number or code to check the registry with?"

Ensign Dar said, "Yes sir. The code that's on the side is, P87E4306-36."

"Hold on a minute while we check," Frank said motioning toward the navigator.

"The ship belongs to Kamon freights. Status: Inactive."

"Then it is a derelict," Matt said somehow pleased. "Come on home, ensign. We'll monitor the situation from the bridge."

"Aye, aye, captain. Over and out," the ensign said.

Everything went quite pleasant on the Orion for the next couple of hours. Matt was on the bridge, where he should be, talking to various crew members about their departments' research and respective angle on the problem before them. All other personnel around the bridge, and perhaps the entire ship, were doing their best to try and work on a way either to reach an agreement with the captures or a way to storm the building and safely arrest them.

Everything was discussed, could be this, may be that, probably this, probably that. This thing came before that thing. The absolute contexts may have been different, but they were

all the same as far as the could
be's, maybe's, and everything else.

Everything was quite par for the
course. The Orion's patrol may not
have brought forth the same magnitude
of problems before the crew, but the
crews were all the same on those
issues too.; could be this, may be
that, probably this, probably that.

The crew members were taught all
throughout school to deal with
educated guessing. There weren't too
many things for certain in the
universe. ...mathematics, history,
etc... But even those were littered
with education guessing. This theory
versus that theory, we think this
was, we think that was, this was this
man's motivation, we think, this
officer thought this, we think. It
was all subjective.

Matt had always found such things
as an irony in society. Sometimes
this theory would prove the best
choice, sometimes not. The trick in
life, he thought, is to read between
the theories. Go directly for what
you were after and meet your goals
head on. Live your dreams, don't
become a victim of them. Maintain a
good balance between safety and

security because nothing in this world is certain.

"Message coming in captain," Melanie said, as Craig stepped out of the turbovator and headed toward his science station to the right of the captain.

"Is it the reconnaissance party," Matt asked.

Melanie responded, "No sir. It's from Mr. Cartier."

"Put it on the main viewscreen Lieutenant," Matt said as he noticed Craig heading towards his general science station, probably to monitor the automatic sensors.

Melanie nodded and worked with several buttons on her console. The image of Cartier on the viewscreen immediately followed her actions.

"Good day to you sir," Matt greeted.

"Hello, Captain Roberts. You're probably wondering why I'm calling," Joe Cartier said.

Matt, apparently puzzled, scratched his head and said, "Why, yes, frankly, I am, Joe."

Craig looked up from his instruments to monitor Cartier's

words because he knew along with the rest of the bridge crew that even the most insignificant thing could prove to be an instrumental key for diffusing a situation.

"Well, I noticed we seem to have had quite a delay between our first meeting and our second," Cartier said. "My understanding was that Ted would relate what has been discussed, that you and your crew would brief Ted further, and then you would come back for another session.. May I ask why you're delaying?"

"Well sir," Matt said, "it's going takes quite a bit of time to rest up after each session. We don't discuss much with Ted the pertinent matters. He already knows where we stand. But flying time is involved, which is very difficult on me. I have to rest, Ted has to rest, the crew has to brief me on all the ship's matters, there are loads of other things."

Cartier paused a moment to think of a resolution, then smiled and said, "Well captain, if your second in command can handle the ship's affairs, I suggest you and Ted stay down here. That would cut out a lot of the things you mentioned. If you need to talk to your ship at any time, I can arrange privacy and a secure and encrypted channel to your ship."

Matt's mouth bulged from being held tight, his eyebrows bulged too, in a downward direction. Matt's speech seemed drawn out when he said, "I don't know if that's such a good idea. My commander is fairly new to the Orion and much of his experience has come from the maintenance detail that's he's been on."

Craig decided to break in. "Captain," Matt, Frank, Cartier, and, in fact, the entire bridge crew, looked over toward Craig as he spoke. "I quite agree with Mr. Cartier. You looked extremely tired when you and Ted arrived. I haven't seen Ted recently, so I assume he's still sleeping. I can help Frank over any rough spots. I strongly suggest that you think about this carefully."

Matt looked at Craig, carefully thinking over what he had said. Looking back at the viewscreen, and thereby Cartier, he said, "I accept your hospitality, Joe. One thing I would like to ask though."

"Name it," Cartier said.

"I'd like one room with two beds and no guards for 25 yards in any direction."

"I can't promise that 100 percent of the time. What I can do is give you a soundproof isolation chamber whenever you communicate with your ship or talk to Ted about the negotiations." Cartier said proudly.

"That will be satisfactory Joe," said Matt.

The viewscreen went blank after Melanie O'hara pushed a few buttons on her control panel. Matt looked anxious as he was squirming in his big armed captain's chair as if in apprehension about the upcoming stay on the planet's surface. Craig went back to his monitoring of sensors while Frank left the bridge to catch up on some of his left over maintenance duties.

All was quiet again on the bridge. Matt was busily starting to check the work of his bridge officers in order to more familiarize himself with the inner workings of the ship he would soon lose. He liked the command of a vessel in the Space

Patrol, but it couldn't help him with his problem.

He had advanced to the very pinnacle of what he aspired in his youth. Where do you go when you've reached every career goal that you've ever set for yourself? The very question he had wrestled with for years.

Matt got up from his chair and started toward the turbovator.

"Hey captain, where are you going," Craig asked as the movement caught his attention.

Matt, with hands that were flexing, replied, "To Ben's office to see if he has any listening devices that we haven't tried. We've only tried one type, there's bound to be a host of others."

"Great idea," Craig said, "Would you mind if I tag along?"

"Not at all, Craig," Matt said with his arm now in mid-air. The fingers on his hand were pointed up and moving back and forth in symbolism of what he said.

The two men stepped on the turbovator and with Matt's utterance of the deck he wanted, the doors closed.

The normal chit-chat that was usually to be found in this spacious area was not to be found among the men. The turbovator stopped to let a dark haired man and a blonde, thin, woman on. Both of them had electronic clipboards in their hands. "Hello, captain," came a comment from the middle aged man.

"Hello, crewman, hard at work on our problems, I see," said Matt as he eyed the clipboard in the ensign's hand.

The turbovator began moving again as the young man answered his captain's query. "Yes, sir. We're coming up with some very interesting things."

"I bet so. Keep up the good work you two," said Matt closing out the discussion.

The turbovator stopped again before the ensign could answer. As Craig and Matt began stepping off the ensign said, "Oh, we will, sir."

Matt and Craig took a left turn in the corridor and immediately following, a right turn. Midways down the adjoining corridor they turned in Ben's office. Ben was standing to the right of the room trying to sort through the library of disc's they had of the planet.

"Hello Ben," Matt said.

Ben stopped handling the disc's for a moment to say, "Hello, captain, what can I do for you today?"

Matt watched as Ben finished gathering up the disc's that he needed while saying, "I thought I would come down to see if you could give me some eavesdropping devices."

Ben's face elongated, cheeks up and eyebrows the same. "I thought that was to be handled the night before a conference, to slip one or two on Ted while he slept."

In surprise at himself, Matt's face gave an almost parallel expression of surprise. He remembered only the bridge crew knew of his new place of residence (at least for the meantime). "I greatly apologize. Let me fill you in." Matt proceeded to tell Ben of what had just happened on the bridge. He ended up his story by saying, "And I want some eavesdropping devices to try while we're there."

After hearing Matt's tale, Ben said with pride, "Of course captain. I've got many different types of listening devices; some of which me and my department have created. Come back here I'll show you some." Upon finishing his statement and request, Ben walked toward a dark blue doorway in the back of the room, opened the door, and led the men in.

The huge room was filled with an arsenal of weapons, tactical devices, explosives, and a host of other things. Craig thought that this one room must have took up twenty-percent of the ship. If the Orion's crew had to resort to a ground assault it was intended for them to win, that was for sure.

Ben was busily weaving his way through the equipment saying, "Right this way, gentleman." He turned this way, that way, right turn, left turn………… Craig wondered where all this was leading. Just how much combat gear could there be?

It was all very neatly stacked though. Each section was squared off from the rest of the equipment. Each square was about 20' x 20', enough to hold all the equipment for one squad

of men. They would have everything
they needed: ammunition, firearms,
medical supplies, and way to get
around whatever terrain they happened
to find themselves in.

Stopping in front of a glass
cabinet to his left, Ben said, "This
is it guys. The pie'sta re'sistance."
As the three men looked down into the
glass pane one could see the light in
their eyes. It was one of curiosity.

"Well," Matt said, "which ones
should we try?"

Ben began lifting up the glass
pane saying, "We could try them all,
but that would be impractical. I
mean, there are so many. Besides,
shielding that many bugs from their
scanners would prove impossible. I
could give you, like, a dozen at a
time."

Ben gathered up a dozen of the
ones he thought had the most chance
for success. "Here you go," said Ben
as he put the devices into a black,
leather looking sack with shiny metal
seams. "These will get you started.
When you plant these little devices
on Ted use this insertion tool." Ben
held up a small device, which
resembled a laser pistol, but was

much slimmer. "The devices can be inserted anywhere on the body, but preferably in the arms or legs," Ben said as he dropped the devices in the black bag.

"I recommend inserting them two at a time, just like we planned," Ben continued. "Each device has its respective strengths and weaknesses. Using them in conjunction with one another, who knows we may get lucky. We know which devices you have, so at the start of each new day we'll just scan the frequencies of the devices until we get a signal." Pausing a moment, Ben added, "Oh, and the bag shields the devices from sensors, so you shouldn't have any trouble."

Matt took the bag from Ben's hand and said, "Thank you for your help, Ben. Now if you would be so kind as to guide us out of here, I'll go to my cabin and rest some before Ted and I make the trip back down to the planet."

"Of course, captain," Ben said, "Follow me." Back they went to the central room of the tactical advisors. The scenery was the same, just from a different angle. It was kind of breathtaking actually. To think that people built these things, these machines, all this technology was developed over eons. There were principles involved here that dated back to old Earth. These things were truly a marvel of modern technology. These were time machines.

They quickly reached the office from which they entered the ship's arsenal. Craig quickly said goodbye and good luck to his captain and went to perform some research. Matt, with the black bag in his left hand, trailed off to the turbovator, went down to his quarters, and packed his white, cloth bag with the things he would need on the planet.

When he got through, he sat down at his terminal and reached into the black bag that Ben gave him, and with the optical coding that was on the rear of the listening devices, began researching the strengths and weaknesses of each device. Inserting a disc into the terminal he was sure to save each set of data on the disc.

When he was through with all the devices, he put them all back in the sack and took the disc out of the terminal. He put the disc in the bag

with all the devices. He got up from
the hard backed chair and commenced
to lay down on his bed. In five
minutes Matt was asleep.

CHAPTER 14

After Matt woke up from his nap,
he called Ted's cabin to wake him up.
Ted was groggy after spending part of
the night with the facilitation
device that Polly had loaned to him.
After hearing from Matt, via
intercom, that he was going to stay
on the planet during the rest of the
negotiations, he quickly grabbed the
clothes that the medical staff had
requisitioned for him, stuffed them
in a shiny, black bag, clutched the
bag in his right hand, and headed out
of the door toward the shuttle bay.

He quickly arrived at the door,
and was about to enter, when he saw
Matt approaching from the corridor
directly in front of him.

Ted greeted his fellow rider with
a wave of his left hand. Oral
communication would been difficult
because of the distance between them.
Instead of waiting for any response,
Ted headed on into the shuttle bay.
As his forward motion was directed
towards the door, the door quickly
separated itself at the middle,
leaving a fully open doorway.

When Matt arrived at the door, he entered as Ted had, and saw the huge inner rectangular, inner folds of the shuttle bay.

There was a nearby shuttle with hoses attached to it which, evidently, was meant for Matt and Ted. Ted was standing near the door talking briefly to one of shuttle technicians.

Matt walked over to the two men and issued his greeting to the technician. "What are you two discussing?"

"Oh, just this, that, and the other thing, just general chit-chat," the technician said.

"Is the shuttle ready to go? Evidently not," said Matt scowling.

The technician started explaining, "We're refueling and calibrating some of the onboard ...."

Matt interrupted, "Just will we be able to take off on schedule?"

"Yes, sir," the technician replied.

"Good," said Matt. "Let's get onboard Ted."

"All right, Matt," said Ted, hoping no one heard him slip up.

Matt and Ted got on the shuttle and nestled into the seats that they had familiarized themselves with on the last trip. Of course, this probably wasn't the same shuttle, not with as many of them the Orion had, but all the shuttles had the same type of seats.

A few minutes after the had each plopped down in their chairs, there was a loud click and Matt said, "Pre-flight check done and door electronically sealed." He had done his preparation swiftly. Too swiftly for the ground crew, in fact...

"Just a moment captain, we're still disconnecting hoses from the shuttle," came a voice from the shuttle's loudspeaker.

The next few seconds couldn't go by too quickly for Matt. He wanted to get underway. He wanted to exploit this time in history.

"Opening bay doors," came the voice from the control tower.

The shuttle starting rising as the doors were opening. It peeped its head out of the bay just as the bay doors were fully open. The stars seemed beautiful to Matt. It was his lifelong dream to be among them. Oh,

the many worlds he had seen were all
pretty, but Matt always thought that
this area in space was the prettiest.
The sky was littered with stars here,
and they seemed to be much brighter
than any area he'd ever been in.
Plus, there was a nearby nebula that
gave the sky the appearance of glazed
streaks.

In comparison to the scenery
around the shuttle, it was very tiny,
a factor that always irritated Matt.
In all of his escapades, he had
always found that intelligent life,
such as humanoids, were always,
roughly speaking, the same size. As
the shuttle entered the atmosphere
Matt wondered, once again, why that
was so. It seemed like the tinier the
brain, the less of an ability to
adapt. Speech, which evolved as a
necessity, was just such an example.
If dogs had a need for speech, which
to him seemed evident, why didn't
they evolve it: they were less
adaptable. One thing he knew for
certain, he was going to adapt.

The shuttle set down on the
landing pad once more. This time Matt
was able to compensate for the higher

gravity quite well and the shuttle
set down smoothly on the landing
area. When the two men felt the ship
had reached a standstill, Matt undid
the locks on the shuttle door. The
two men unstrapped themselves and
walked out of the shuttle. The same
two men as before were waiting
outside for them.

The tall, blonde, man said,
"Follow me, Ted. Mr. Cartier is
waiting for you."

As the blonde started to lead Ted
towards Cartier, the dark haired man
with a heavy build inched closer to
Matt saying, "Follow me and I'll show
you where you will stay."

Matt, thinking that Ted was out
hearing range, said with an eager
voice, "Beware of the second
transmitter." With that said, he
handed the big man a disc.

CHAPTER 15

On the bridge, Craig was checking in with the ship's tactical experts, psychologists, and the communications officer, Melanie O'hara, who was monitoring communications. Nobody seemed to know a damn thing. It was like the whole situation was being smothered with a blanket.
...Listening devices, sensors, grounds people, surveys, nothing was getting them anywhere...

"Incoming communication from Admiral Rutherford," Melanie said in Craig's direction.

Craig broke his conversation with one of the bridge crew short and said, "Since Commander Doan is not here, I guess I'll answer it Lieutenant."

"On screen, sir," Melanie said.

The main viewscreen lit up once again with the image of the admiral. "Lt. Commander Craig Holt, here, admiral. Go ahead."

"Where is your exec's Mr. Holt," said the admiral raising an eyebrow.

"Captain Roberts is staying on the planet's surface for the duration of the negotiations and Commander

Doan is on one of lower decks reviewing the data logs from a reconnaissance mission," Craig said with some apprehension.

The admiral looked dismayed. "What's going on that would need a reconnaissance for?"

"Well, sir, our sensors picked up a freighter in orbit around the 12th planet in this system. We investigated it and found it to be, apparently, a derelict. We're keeping an eye on it though," said Craig.

"Well Mr. Holt, I have not received a progress report at any time. Has Captain Roberts been back aboard at any time," Admiral Rutherford asked, growing more impatient.

Craig hated to answer that question, because he knew what would follow his statement. "Yes, sir. He has. I'm not sure what the delay has been."

"What the heck has been going on out there?"

Craig decided that honesty was his best defense. "Admiral, I don't know what to say.............. Allow me to fill you in. First of all, do you know about the life pod we intercepted?"

The admiral nodded and said, "Yes I do."

"Do you know of his true identity?"

"Unfortunately I do."

"Do you know he's become the only negotiator that Cartier would accept," Craig asked.

"What," exclaimed the admiral with a loud voice. "How can that be? Weren't precautions taken?"

"Yes, sir," Craig said sheepishly. Unwillingly, at this point, to admit his investigation of the incident, Craig said, "Somehow Cartier knew that Ted was onboard, or maybe he saw him somewhere."

"I supposed Matt suspended Ted's memory recall program," the admiral stated, questioningly.

"Yes, sir, immediately." Craig paused for a moment. The admiral did too. Craig included in his report his advisement that Ted and Matt stay on the surface and the listening devices Ben had given to Matt.

"That's fine," the admiral said wearily. "I'd rather it not be one,

but it's probably for the better. Any
good news?"

Craig didn't want to answer that
question either. "No, sir, we've done
a lot of research, but all we come up
with are more questions."

The admiral, surprisingly, didn't
let that upset him. "Well, this is a
complex, delicate situation. The crew
will eventually come up with
something. Tell your commander to
check in more frequently. Rutherford
out."

Having hidden two transmitters on
Ted, Frank, Craig, and Ben, who were
sitting at the center of the table,
thought they were almost guaranteed
of success. The viewscreen in front
of them was filled with a picture of
Ted walking down one of the hallways
in the capitol building. It was the
same lavishly decorated room that
they were viewing before; gold trim
on the elegantly molded door frames,
corner braces of elegant design, a
paradigm of beauty.

The three men watched with great
anticipation. Feeling almost that
they had outsmarted Cartier and The
Pak was most of it. Reversion back to

their youth was the other part. Every kid had that sneaky suspicion that he knew what he was getting for Christmas, a promise of the unknown. The unknown aspect of anything held a keen interest for a person and especially for a kid. A kid is learning so much, he doesn't know what to expect. He strives to learn more through self-propulsion.

Interest in the unknown... That is the key.

Ben mostly watched the device to his lower left. It showed the layout of the area 50 yards around where Ted was. Walls were predominantly what it indicated, but an occasional desk and chair were in there too.

The picture slowly started to show interference. The picture was getting filled with white blotches and some distortion. The sensor net and audio began to go blank and silent as well. The buildup was slow and gradual, but eventually everything was shut down.

A metal conduit, or static discharge was hopefully the problem. Anxiously, the three men waited for the interference to pass, especially being that there was little else they could do. Everything came back to them, sensor net, audio, and video, as slowly as it faded.

Immediately following, there was another surge of interference. Slowly, everything came back. There was another and another and another and then the transmission went away for good.

There was a moment of silence in the room, then Craig said, "Switch to second transmitter Ben."

Heartily agreeing what Craig said, Ben said, "Righto!"

It was for nothing though. The other transmitter had gone dead also.

"Damn it," Ben shouted, "Every damn time. It's like something is fighting us. We still haven't got a damn clue."

Frank, trying to calm Ben down, said, "Patience. We're bound to get lucky sometime."

"Well I'm tired of waiting," Ben said. "Something has gotta happen soon."

"I know, I know," Craig said.

Frank pushed his hands on the table in front of him and raised his buttocks out of the chair that he had been sitting in. "Well gentleman, shall we adjourn ourselves?"

Ben, still seated, said, "Can anyone think of anything else to try? I mean the transceivers are getting us no place."

"I'm open to suggestions," Frank said.

"Any action we take," Craig said, "will be readily observed by the planetary defense system. Without knowing what the scrambled frequency is, we can't thwart its mechanisms. Essentially, we're stuck."

"I guess you're right," Ben reluctantly admitted to himself. "I knew that, but I was hoping we could devise an alternate plan."

"Such as," Frank said.

"I'm not sure," Ben said.

"I share your opinions, Ben," Frank said. "But until we devise a plan we're stuck, as Craig said. Work on it. You're the best man for the job."

Ben, finally standing up, said, "Okay, I will."

After the botched eavesdropping effort, Craig hurried down to the computer department. He was hoping that she would take some time to, again, work together with him. He had done a awful lot of research on Ted, but had come up empty. He was hoping she had had better luck.

As he walked in, he was almost run over by one of the technicians. Moving quickly he stepped to one side to let the busy woman by. Seeing Jane through the transparent walls of the outer room in front of her office, he opened the door and said, "Hey, lovely thing. Mind if I come in?"

Although Craig had interrupted Jane's giving instructions to her office mate, Jane quickly finished her oratory and enthusiastically replied, "Hello, pal of mine. Come into my parlor please."

Following her precocious stride through the office door, Craig eagerly followed. Once they were inside and the door was closed, Craig gave her a deep look,, as if he were trying to see her thoughts. "Could you come up with anything on what we discussed," he asked.

Jane shook her head and slumped a tad as she said, "I'm afraid not. I've put in a lot of time researching it too. Whoever is trying to hide, sure knows their stuff."

"You mean even the automatic computer log didn't have anything," Craig asked, as if in shock.

"No. The whole thing is baffling."

"Apparently this incident is covered too well to be retrieved. Let's check other things, any anomalies................," Craig said.

"Craig, dear, maybe there is no cover up."

Craig, with eyes wide and eyebrows raised, said, "Maybe so, but I'd still like to look at all the logs and check out any anomalies."

Jane, in a show of resignation, sighed. "Okay, whatever you say."

"Let's look at the communication logs first that would be the most clear cut evidence of foul play," said Craig.

"Okay. I have a little time," said Jane as she pointed the chair under her desk toward the terminal on her desktop. The screen lit up with a schedule of communications to and from the ship. "These are the transmissions from the day that Cartier came aboard," she said.

They both gazed at the screen, soaking in every detail as a starving animal eats all the food he can find. It was several minutes before they each concluded that what they were seeking wasn't there.

Craig said, "Let's look back a few days."

Jane pressed a few keys and some more information lit up the screen. After a minute of scouring Jane said, "Same thing, honey. No anomalies."

The same thing happened to them again and again. A list of transmission would come up, but nothing was odd about the list. Jane had long given up hope of finding anything. She knew she had put a lot of her time and efforts in this project. She was the one person that should have been able to find anything out of the ordinary. Craig knew that too, but still he insisted on continuing. He had learned to trust his instincts and they told him something skrewy was going on.

"Wait!" Craig quickly pointed to the screen at a call made from the Orion at 2:37am. "Could we replay this call?"

Jane hesitated before answering. "I can, but I can't let you see it. It could mean my job."

"I can wait in the outer office," a frustrated Craig said .

"Okay. I'll come get you in minute and relate anything important," said Jane.

"Okay," Craig said. He then turned around and marched toward the door saying, "See you in a minute."

It was a long while before Jane called Craig back into her office. When she stuck her head out of her office door, she appeared a bit shaky. Her body movements were slightly erratic and not very smooth, as a confident person's would be.

Jane guarded the door as Craig entered, making certain to close it immediately after his body had cleared the brink of the door.

"What's wrong," Craig asked staring at her.

"I think you ought to see this for yourself," Jane responded. Replacing herself in front of her terminal, she began to type and said, "The call was encrypted, that's one reason why it took so long."

Following her keystrokes, the
message began to play. The screen was
split in half by a white, vertical
line. On the left side of the screen
was the an image of Matt; on the
right was the image of Cartier.

Cartier: "Hello"
Matt: "We have a problem
to discuss. Peter is here. We
picked him up in a life pod and
               has amnesia."
Cartier: "That is a big
problem. We need those   weapons
that were on that ship."
Matt: "I know."
(pause)
Cartier: "Maybe we can
salvage this thing anyway.
               Maybe I can
negotiate with him instead   of
you."
Matt: "That's possible. I
can arrange for you   to spot him
when you come aboard. Then   you
can demand to negotiate with
him."
Cartier: "Sounds good to me.
Then we can just follow through
with the rest of the plan."

     Matt: "Sounds good. I'll
see you then."
     Cartier: "See you then."

     Craig just stood in shock at what
he had heard. He knew now why Jane
had looked so shaky, because he too
was shaken. After a few moments, he
regained his senses and said, "Would
you put that on a disc?"

CHAPTER 16

"Calling Commander Doan," Craig said into the intercom on the wall inside the computer center.

Frank's voice came over Craig's intercom speaker. "Frank Doan here."

"Frank, you need to meet me in the main conference room as soon as you can," Craig said.

Realizing the sense of urgency in Craig's words, Frank said, "I'll be right there, Craig."

With his compatriot on his way, Craig headed straight to the conference room. With legs pounding the floor like the fast beat of a drummer pounding on a bass drum, he marched quickly towards his destiny. His body was busily pumping adrenaline through his body, which made Craig feel light headed and gave him a headache.

Although the effort of his walking down the hallway gave his body an outlet, the adrenal pumped up his body too much for mere walking to dissipate. He began thinking of all the enjoyable times he and Matt had had together. Oh, the many wonderful times they had had, and he remembered all the great conversations they used to have in the many diners aboard the ship. Matt had asked for Craig onboard the Orion, got him transferred there, and subsequently developed a great relationship with him.

Craig felt betrayed by, practically, the only person in Star Patrol that had ever given him a break. 'Why would a man befriend you and then set you and the others onboard up to fail,' he thought. 'How could he do that?'

Reaching the conference room in record time, Craig saw that he had beaten Frank. He thought about inserting the disc that Jane had given him into the player, but he did not want to let it out of his sight until he was ready to demonstrate it. He began pacing around the conference table to settle his nerves. It did not help.

When Frank walked in Craig thought, 'Finally.' "Frank, I need to show you something that I found."

"Go ahead," Frank said, unaware of the gravity of the subject matter.

"This matter is of an extremely important nature and could be very unsettling," Craig said.

"O-kay," Frank said.

Craig put the disc in the player and the events that had unfolded in Jane's office were revealed to Frank. Stunned, after it got through playing he was silent a moment. After he regained his senses, Frank asked, "What should we do?"

"Maybe we can use him," Craig said with a slight tilt of his head.

"I don't know. I just don't know. How?" Frank said shaking his head.

"By letting him think we're not onto him so we can feed him dummy information," said Craig.

"I'm not sure I would be good at that," Frank said.

"You have to be convincing, Frank. You have to be a leader or else lots of people will die," Craig said strongly.

Frank looked uncertain of himself and said, "I've only been aboard eight months and most of that has been on maintenance detail."

Craig looked at Frank with cold, glaring eyes, "Frank, if you don't think you can handle this, you need to do something about it. Until then, I can only advise and give you the benefit of my skills."

"Under ordinary circumstances, yes, I could handle the ship," Frank said. "But," he added, "the circumstances are far from normal, and I don't want to jeopardize lives or the mission."

Craig, puzzled, replied, "Then what do you intend on doing?"

Frank's answer was immediate and without hesitation. "I have the power to promote some else to the rank of commander. The rank will be subject to approval by a higher ranking officer, but it will be valid until then."

Surprised at the answer, and not wanting to argue with a superior officer, Craig said, "Very well. Who?"

"Nobody is as close to the situation as you, Ben, and me, and I think Ben is too volatile for the job."

"I think he is too," said Craig solemnly, but with glee in his heart.

Frank placed his right arm on Craig's left shoulder, and said, "I promote you to the rank of acting commander. I shall enter into the ship's log that you are now commander and I am the general science officer."

"Thank you for your confidence Ben. I shall try not to let you, or the ship, down. For purposes of communicating with Captain Roberts, I hope you will continue to speak as commander?"

"I certainly will."

Craig took his disc out of the terminal and the two men recorded the change of ranks.

After the conversation between Craig and Frank trailed off, collectively, the two men were to locate all the department heads in order to have a conference with them. Frank was assigned the lower deck departments and Craig the upper. Craig had told Ben, Valerie, and was on the last deck, the bridge, when Melanie said, "Incoming transmission."

Craig snapped to attention. "Who is it Ms. O'hara?"

Melanie responded uncertain, "They refuse to identify themselves, but it's on an unusual wavelength, the kind usually meant for commercial use, but very uncommon, and very weak."

"Put it onscreen, Lt.," Craig said.

"Sorry sir, audio only. On speaker sir," Melanie responded apologetically.

"Calling Star Patrol, Calling Star Patrol," the deep voice said.

"This is Star Patrol," Craig said. Careful to avoid the use of his new rank he said, "Craig Holt here."

"I need to make you aware of a situation on Delta Five. The captain of the Star Patrol vessel in orbit here is a traitor. He's sabotaging every effort by the crew to bring a reasonable resolution to the situation here. All the information I have will be transmitted to you using Red Code."

"Who............."

Melanie interrupted Craig. "Transmission cut off, but I'm receiving a Red Code transmission from the planet."

"Ms. O'hara," Craig said, "Pipe that transmission down to the main conference room, still coded. I'll be right down." Looking around the room he continued, "All department heads not critical to the ship's functionality meet me there in 10 minutes."

With ship's records keepers busily handing Craig's electronic reports to sign, Craig was unable to get off the bridge as quickly as he wanted to. Fuel consumption reports, records retrieval requests, approvals galore, it all seemed so needless.

Slowly, the replacement personnel filtered into the workings of the bridge. One by one went the main bridge personnel, sometimes two by two. As Craig was speaking to the one of the records keepers, almost everyone except a few bridge officers and poor Melanie left the bridge. James, Pete, Scott, and several others had left, but, in a dire situation, good communications between parties were absolutely critical.

Craig got through with all the signing, and finally headed towards the conference room. Everyone else that was going from the bridge had already left.

He stepped near the turbovator door and it parted in the middle to allow his entrance. Inside he pushed the button to indicate the floor and the compartment began moving.

It next opened at his designated floor and he stepped out. The doors closed behind him as he walked down the corridor to his left. Craig walked a fair distance, then turned left again. As he walked he thought about his new rank. He hoped it would be approved by Space Patrol. He was never supposed to able to achieve this rank. The incident when he was younger was supposed to have precluded any possibility of a command rank. That was not important right now though, stopping this situation in its tracks was.

As he rounded the final turn toward the conference room, he saw the door which held his fate. The cold, gray door did not look inviting at all and Craig hoped it wasn't a representation of his future.

In the door he went. The room was filled to capacity with every department head on the huge ship. There were people talking in 6 or 7 groups Craig estimated. 'Well,' Craig

thought, 'it's time.' He marched
stately toward the chair with all the
controls and said, "Will everyone
quiet down." A quick hush fell over
the room.

Craig continued, "I called this
conference to make everyone aware of
some drastic changes," Pause. "About
an hour ago, we decoded a
transmission made by Captain Roberts.
This transmission reveals the
captain's true knowledge about the
man who we have been calling Ted, who
is Peter Topper, by the way. The
captain evidently knew it was Peter
Topper by his working with Cartier
and The Pak. We must now consider the
captain an enemy.

"Peter Topper was delivering
weapons to Cartier when his ship went
haywire. The captain arranged for Ted
to be the negotiating party. We can
only guess they're working with his
memory instead of negotiating."

"Is this confirmed," asked a
crewman.

Craig's answer was, "The contents
of the transmission were
unmistakable."

"Why isn't Commander Doan telling us all this," another a young female lady asked.

"Due to Commander Doan's inexperience, unfamiliarity with the ship and crew, he thought it best if I take over. He promoted me to acting commander and he has temporarily stepped back to general science officer. Any more questions before I continue?"

The silence gave Craig his answer, so he went on. "I think we can use the captain by feeding him non-pertinent details about what we're up to."

Craig paused. "We received a confirming transmission about the captain just minutes ago. It originated from the planet by an unknown person. They transmitted some details about the planet after they broke off communication." Craig looked toward Ben Waters, "Are you ready to present that information, Ben?"

Ben looked up from the terminal and shook his head. "Too quick," he said disappointed in himself.

With hesitation Craig said, "Just give me what you have."

"On the projector, Craig."

The bland colored orb in the center of the elongated conference table started to glow and a three dimensional image that resembled a maze lit up above the table.

"Ben," Craig said, "you better take it from here."

Ben began explaining, "This is a representation of the Alphorzia mines. According to the information we received," Pointing to the reddish dot inside the projection, "these red dots indicate where the bombs are. There are 30 bombs in all scattered throughout the planet, naturally, this is not a representation of them all. The bombs are in contact with a remote switch all the time, via satellite. The moment contact is broken, they explode." Pausing a moment Ben continued, "As yet, that's all the information I've looked at. Unless the commander has anything to add………"

Craig spoke up to say, "I will make a ship-wide announcement in a few minutes. Until then, there will be no discussion among yourselves or the crew. Is that understood?"

A chorus of crew members said, "Yes, sir."

The meeting broke up noisily with sounds of crew member after crew member getting up from their seat, if they were sitting, and exiting through the doorway. Craig was about to turn and go to where Frank was, the bridge, to talk to him. He was halfway around the table when he was met by Valerie's worried face.

"Could I talk to you a minute Craig, in private."

"Sure," Craig said, knowing what was on her mind. "Let's just wait for these people to filter out."

It was very tense as they waited. It was hard on both of them. One by one, they exited. The dispersion of that many people was shorter than they expected. Noticing that the table was roughly hip high Craig raised his buttocks up and over the table in order to sit on it.

When the room had vacated, Craig asked, "What's on your mind?"

Valerie had quit being a doctor at that moment. There were tears in her eyes. And she began asking her question as a woman, "Craig, is there no way this can be wrong about Matt?"

Feeling very sympathetic, Craig said, "I guess both sources could be wrong, but that's not very likely."

"So there is a chance?"

"Yes, but speaking as commander now, I don't think we can afford to risk everything on a minute possibility," Craig responded.

"I agree, but I don't know how I could have been so wrong about Matt."

Craig put his right hand on her left shoulder. "I sympathize with you. I too misjudged him, terribly."

Sobbing, she put her arms around his chest. He, in turn, wrapped her up with his long arms. Reaching over her shoulders, he rubbed her back with short up and down strokes. In the comfort of each others arms, they stood there for a few minutes releasing all their feelings of disappointment and betrayal on one another. When at last they broke up they said a few words of emotional comfort to one another, and then adjourned.

CHAPTER 17

On the bridge, Frank was talking to a young lieutenant about the days events, making sure to exclude the conference. The bridge was a steady bustle of activity: combat trajectories being plotted, ship's defenses being firmed, ground attacks, etc. The steady onslaught of stimulations were staggering.

The turbovator opened in the rear of the bridge and Craig walked through the door as the two halves parted. Frank had his back to the door, sitting in the command chair, and was surprised when Craig came around to right.

Getting up quickly, Frank said, "Hello, Craig."

"Hello, Frank. I have a job for you and Ben. I want you to go to the captain's cabin and search it for anything that might help us know what he's up to," Craig said.

"Will do, sir," Frank said. "Any other orders?"

"Well, if you find anything strange, just deal with it as you think best."

"Okay," Frank replied. Going toward the turbovator, he stopped just short of the doors and pressed the white button for the intercom on the wall. "Calling Ben Waters."

After a moment of silence Ben answered, "Ben here."

"Meet me at the captain's cabin."

"I'll be right there," Ben said.

"See you there," Frank said. He walked through the gray doors of the turbovator immediately afterward.

After Frank left, Craig signaled Melanie to put him on ship wide intercom by saying, "Ms. O'hara, I have a statement to issue to the crew."

"Intercom ready, commander," Melanie said after she fidgeted with her controls.

"Attention crew, this is Acting Commander Holt. I must make you aware of certain events that are happening aboard the ship for our mission to go smoothly.

"First, Captain Roberts has been found to be a traitor. He's been working with our enemy for quite some time. In view of this, we cannot afford to communicate with Star

Patrol at any time, or in any way, until our mission is complete. All external communication access points will hereby be locked out except for here on the bridge."

Taking a moment to swallow and slightly wet his dry throat, Craig continued, "Secondly, Until this mission is complete, I am the new commander due to Frank Doan's lack of experience.

"People, we are in a bad situation here, so I expect every crew member to give this situation every single bit of effort that it deserves, and demands. That is all.

Craig looked around the room, straight into the eyes of everyone on the bridge. Most of them were of sterling character and did not back away from his stare. Craig was trying to see whether they had confidence in his abilities to lead them in a critical situation such as this.

Turning the command chair around so he could do that was as easy as walking, but he was surprised at how slow he went. Perhaps it was his own uneasiness that delayed him.

He was pleased to find that the crew had rigid eyes, a look of

confidence. Oh, there was a look or
two of nervousness and uncertainty,
but overall, they look confidant. The
young crew members would perform
according to their abilities or just
play a game of 'Follow The Leader.'

Finally, breaking the air of
silence that surrounded the bridge,
Craig said, "Well Ms. O'hara, you
heard the order on communications."

Melanie said, "Yes, sir. I'll put
that lockout on communications right
away."

"As for the rest of the bridge
crew, when and if the captain makes a
check in with us, for his purposes
Frank is still the commander and I am
still the general science officer.
With that being the order, and since
we can't afford a slip up, from now
until the end of this mission the
entire bridge crew is permanently
stationed here. You will work, eat,
and sleep here."

The bridge's metal walls
shuddered with the statement, as a
person's nerves might make their legs
shake. Everyone wasn't concerned
about being on duty, but of making a
mistake.

Ben saw Frank finally traipsing down the hallway. He had been waiting on him for a long while. He was irritated too. He had been correlating data from the transmission and dropped everything to come meet Frank. He didn't know why Craig wanted him to come, he didn't even know what was planned, but it must have been pretty important. For something important like that it should been a priority for Frank.

Running down the corridor, Frank called out, "Hey, Ben."

"Hey," Ben yelled.

Reaching where Ben was, Frank bent down and put his hands on his knees. Out of breathe he said pantingly, "Ah, I got here as quick as I could. Turbovator 8 got stuck."

"Think nothing of it," Ben said. "I was wondering what happened though."

About to catch his breath, Frank said, "Well, that was it my friend. Are you ready?"

"Ready for what," Ben asked.

"We're supposed to search the captain's cabin for anything that might help us?"

"Oh," said Ben realizing the importance of the assignment. "Sure I'm ready."

Frank was the first to enter. "Lights," he said. The large room got bright. He began searching the captain's data recorder. He instructed it to play back the captain's log as they searched.

"… According to star charts …" it said.

Meanwhile, Ben was turning up the captain's bed. The cover went this way, the mattress the other. Pillow ripped to shreds … Mattress ripped apart …

"… This indicates …" the log said.

Frank, looking at the computer disc's that were by the terminal was looking at one of Matt's old letters to a girlfriend. "This is trash," he whispered to himself.

"… Time period on the planet is …" the log said.

Ben saw the pictures on the wall, but was going to save that for last, when he was tired. Instead, he went for the closet. A bunch of the uniforms and other necessities the captain had packed for his stay on

the planet were missing. There were a
few things to search through.

"... Coordinates are ..." the log
said.

Frank had finished searching the
data recorder and went for the
pictures. Unlike Ben, he was looking
for the easy things first. He first
took all the pictures down. He then
examined them one by one. Nothing in,
around, or behind the first two...
Nor the second two... Nor the last
one...

"... Azimuth is ..." the log said.

Spotting a box in the bottom of
the closet, Ben reached and grabbed
it. Opening it up, he saw a pair of
shoes. He went to put it back and
noticed it didn't sit level. He
picked it up, turned it over, and saw
an electronic device.

"... Solar wind is rising ..." the
log said.

"Hey Frank, look at this," Ben
said.

Frank said, "What is that?"

"I'm not exactly sure," Ben said,
"but I think it may be a bomb."

Frank was near the desk where the
terminal and hit the intercom button

that was there. "Calling Acting
Commander Craig."

"… Log books are …"

A voice over the intercom said,
"Craig here."

"Commander, we found a device of
some type in the captain's cabin. Ben
here thinks it may be a bomb."

"Ask Ben if he can arrange a
remote control shuttle," Craig said.

Frank looked at Ben who was
already nodding. "He says that he
can."

"Just send it off to an
uninhabited planet in this system
then. We don't have time to worry
about the loss of one shuttle. And
then get to the conference room for
our plans to storm the planet," Craig
said.

"Okay Craig," Frank said. Frank
clicked off the intercom and the log,
then helped Ben carry the small thing
down to the starboard side, top of
wing, shuttle bay.

As Frank placed it in the floor
of a personal transport shuttle, Ben
set up a control for remote flying.
It was a small gray device with a
black digital facing combined with
light emitting indicators. It

attached under the front of the control panel.

"All right, let's get out of here Frank. We'll send this baby on its way to deep space. The Orion should act as a shield from the planet's sensor's."

They both exited the shuttle bay in favor of its control tower.

"Commencing pre-launch checks," Ben said. Like a skilled mechanic, he carefully experimented with the controls. When he was satisfied that everything was in its proper order he said, "Decompressing … Opening bay doors … Launching shuttle"

The small, metallic shuttle slowly and smoothly lifted off the floor of the bay. Up, up, up, it went, straight through the opening at the top of the shuttle bay.

Ben stepped to his right a tad to quickly program the autopilot onboard the shuttle to maintain the cover of the Orion. Then he and Frank left the shuttle bay in favor of the conference.

CHAPTER 18

"Please settle down," Craig said
in the conference room.

Those that had seats, sat down,
those that didn't got quiet and
still. Craig didn't want to start the
whole thing without Ben, but time
constraints gave him no choice. The
more time they delayed the invasion,
the less of an advantage they would
have and the greater the chance that
they would slip up and let on that
they knew about Matt and the spy.

Craig said, "Lieutenant Rigger,
would you start in the absence of
Ben."

The blonde hair, scraggly voiced
lieutenant replied, "Yes, sir." He
unsteadily began by pushing a button
on the control panel that was mounted
on the table. The orb on the table
glowed and a full diagram of the
tunnels and its access points were
projected into the room.

"Now these are the mining
tunnels, greatly scaled down of
course," the lieutenant indicated.
"The red dots illustrate where the
bombs are. What we've determined is,
since these things are in constant

contact with the detonation device, we can't disarm them."

The lieutenant felt more confidence in himself as he pushed another button to show an image of the planet, its satellites, and its moons. Seeing the image, he continued, "What we can do instead, is control the bombs through the satellites in orbit about the planet. As we said before the bombs are tied together with the master control via the satellites.

"The moment the signal is interrupted via the control, the bombs explode. Thanks to the spy we know the frequency that the control is transmitting. We can feed a false signal to the satellites and thereby take his threat away.

"There are bomb guardians stationed near each bomb for a manual detonation, if need be. We've got to get those guardians out of there, before we invade the complex. If we don't, then we've got trouble. Luckily, if one bomb explodes, the rest don't automatically follo…………"

There was the metallic sound of a door opening from the back of the room and in walked Frank and Ben.

Lieutenant Rigger called to Ben, "Ben, I just finished explaining about the bombs in the mines and the guardians. I haven't told them the about the locations of the guardians. Would you like to take over?"

Stepping aside automatically, the lieutenant sat down as Ben went up to the controls. Ben pressed another button on the panel and a flat projection of the entire planet was shown.

Ben cleared his throat and then said, "The red dots you see and the coordinates beside them indicate where the guardians are. We've got to get them all, quickly and quietly, otherwise they'll likely notify their home base and we'll have a harder time of it."

Pushing a button to make the next projection come up, he continued, "This is obviously the complex where the tower is. The five red dots …" Looking over toward Lieutenant Rigger, Ben asked, "I thought we decided the westerly access was here?" He pointed to a wing on the building that did not have a red marker.

"The lieutenant said, "We decided from the description that he was referring to the northwest wing."

Ben replied, "There are no statues on the west?"

"No, sir."

"Okay, I knew it was a big question."

Continuing with his speech, Ben continued, "The five red dots indicate the weak points in their defenses. Using our armament, we'll go in at these points, but we'll need to have these six other yellow areas fortified in order to achieve containment. Commander …" Ben stepped back and waved his hand at Craig indicating for him to speak again.

Craig got up from his chair and said to Ben, "Thank you, Ben. I commend you and your staff for being able to work so quickly." Looking back toward the crowd of people he continued, "We can't afford to let Cartier slip away; that's one reason why we're being so thorough. Once inside the complex, the troops will have to do as they think best since the spy had the floorplan but didn't know where they were centralized."

Craig looked out at the many faces, trying to memorize them all before the battle began. "People, some of our young men and women might not make it through this. You may not even live through it. But this fight has to be fought and if each and every one of us does his or her best, then we all have a better chance of survival. You, me, everybody...

After the conference, Craig and Frank headed back to the bridge while Ben and his staff coordinated with other departments to get everyone into position. Craig hoped it would not take long to get ready to storm the complex and take the guardians out, but one never knew.

"I think it may go okay," Frank said to Craig in the turbovator.

"Maybe so," Craig said. "I just hope so."

As the turbovator marched onward, crew members entered and exited at a frightening pace. Everyone was making preparations for the future onslaught. Yet, something was very calming about it all. Perhaps Craig was thinking about the many

precautions that were being taken, or
maybe it was something else.

The turbovator stopped at the
bridge finally and the two men
exited. The bridge too seemed to have
the eerie calm that the rest of the
ship had. Everyone was busily
working, including Frank who was
already at Craig's science station,
but things didn't seem quite right
somehow.

Certain members of the bridge
crew were eating, or drinking cups of
coffee. How serene things seemed, to
be totally upside down. He thought
maybe he too, should eat, given the
fact that he hadn't touched a bite of
food since that morning.

"Ensign Clark, would you go to a
cafeteria and get me a sandwich and
some coffee," Craig asked of an
unbusy man.

"Yes, sir," the lad said as he
jumped up.

"Thank you," said Craig.

As the boyish figure traipsed
toward the door, Craig couldn't help
but wonder how many young men and
women like that would die in the
invasion. It hurt Craig a lot to
think about all those people dying

over an order that he gave. But, unfortunately, without hard orders such as those, the Alliance would not have had its long history of peace.

Everyone that has felt the Alliance's aura of peaceful belonging, knows that there are times when, to maintain peace, you need to become a tiger. 'The Star Patrol is like an avenging angel when it comes to keeping peace in the territories,' Craig thought.

He heard the turbovator doors open behind him and turned his chair to see who it was. It was the ensign carrying his things for him. The ensign handed the white container of food to Craig with his left hand and handed the coffee to him with his right.

"Here you go, sir," the ensign said.

"Thank you, ensign," Craig replied as he set the container of food on his lap, having already set the coffee in the cup holder on the arm of the chair.

He opened the white container on his lap and saw a cheese sandwich on wheat and some artificial chips. 'Not the best, but it'll do,' he thought.

He grabbed several of the chips and began eating. 'Not terribly bad,' Craig thought.

A few minutes after Craig had gotten through eating, Melanie said, "Receiving a coded ground communication, commander."

Craig put his cup of coffee in the holder and said, "Put it on speaker, Lieutenant."

"Commander, this is Ben. We've managed to capture all of the bomb guardians except one. We're trying to chase him down now, but Craig, I don't think we can afford to delay invading the complex any longer."

Craig hurriedly responded, "I agree. Start your invasion of the complex. Craig out.

The room livened up quickly. Every officer around the room knew what was expected of them: constant monitoring, scrutenization, and reports. "Meeting light resistance at attack points 1, 3, and 4. Moderate resistance at points 2 and 5," Frank said.

A rapid paced bridge crew were busily monitoring the invasion. Switching from frequency to frequency to frequency, Melanie looked as if she were in a race for her life. Frantically she struggled to keep up, for if she did not, some of the men might die, like her father.

"Fortification points 4, 5, and 6 are reporting that they are under heavy attack," Melanie said.

"Send some people from fortification point 2 to point 5," Craig said with authority. He took another sip of his coffee in an attempt to still his nerves.

"Resistance mounting at attack point 3. Moderate casualties," Frank said.

"Incoming communication from the captain," Melanie said quickly.

Craig looked at Melanie with a blank expression, as if not surprised. "Put it on the screen lieutenant."

An image of a shocked man came on the screen. With eyes wide enough to make his eye sockets seeming round instead of oval, Matt said, "What in the world is going on up there?"

"I should think that would be obvious captain," responded Craig.

"Where is Frank? Give me Frank," the wild eyed captain said.

"I'm afraid I am the acting commander now. Direct your statements to me," Craig said.

"This invasion is wrong Craig. I've been acting as a double agent. You obviously know of the spy. Well, that's me. Stop this attack," Matt said.

Craig said in a monotone, unbelieving voice, "If that's true, then why did we find a bomb in your room?"

Matt's eyes looked down at the panel that was in front of him and then the screen went snowy. Stars quickly took the place of the snow.

Melanie looked up from her panel and said, "Transmission cut off at the source, commander."

Frank said, "All positions report that opposition is slowly degrading. Ground Commander Ben Waters estimates total control of the complex in one hour."

"Have they ever caught that guardian," Craig asked concerned about the detonation of a bomb.

Frank was unhappy to report, "No, sir. They temporarily lost track of him."

"Hell, I'm going down there.
Prepare a combat shuttle and pilot."

CHAPTER 19

On the planet's surface, Craig grabbed a laser pistol from the miniature armory in the combat shuttle and stepped out. There were people running around everywhere the eye could see in the town near the complex. Craig had instructed the pilot to land near where the last guardian was.

"Wait here for me here," Craig shouted to the pilot from outside the door of the shuttle. Craig closed the door to the shuttle then took off down the street to meet a team member he saw.

Running down the street seemed easy with Craig's adrenaline pumped up to a high level. He reached the team member in, what would considered, record time.

"I'm commander Holt. What's the story on this guy," he asked the team member.

"It's a woman," The man said with a groan. "Every time we get a fix on her, she eludes us again. She's very fast and is able to hide extremely well. We've just been unable to pin her down."

"Where is your search team at now," Craig asked.

"They're searching that abandoned building at the moment," the man said while he pointed to the building in front of him. "I decided to wait out here to see if I could spot where she runs to next time."

"I guess I'll stay out here too. When she appears I'll run after her and you just stay here as a spotter. I think that was a good idea," Craig said.

Time went by slowly as they waited for some sign of progress. Craig thought there must be a detonation switch hidden somewhere nearby for her to try to elude the men from the Orion. If he could only talk to her he might be able to coax it out of her.

Suddenly, they saw a woman, dressed in black, running from the left side of the building. She was headed toward a white fence that was behind the building and Craig starting running at his top speed to intercept her. Instead of running straight toward her, he was plotting an intercept course. She darted to her left and was blocked from Craig's view by a building.

Craig ran behind the building as well, only to discover she was nowhere in sight. As the ground crew came running toward the building, he decided to use the 'spotter technique' and just let the ground crew flush her out.

Craig waited patiently, trying to see every detail of the outside of the building. He peered through the window panes too, trying to see her moving. He could not make out a single detail through the dirty, reflective windows, and that annoyed him.

"Over here," someone yelled from around the corner of the building.

Craig ran to his right toward where the voice sounded. When he got to where he could see around the corner, he saw the woman running toward another building. "Stop," he called out. He tried shooting her with his laser pistol, but his shot was high and behind her. It was lucky for everyone's sake that this was a very unpopulated part of the city, otherwise his shot might have injured someone.

Chasing after her, Craig saw a tree that he could topple in order to block her path. He stopped running, took great aim, and fired. It was a direct hit at the base of the tree, only it fell differently than he'd anticipated: away from her path.

Disappointed, Craig began running again. The men that were searching the building were now pursuing, and gaining on her. Craig was growing near to her also. She was evidently tiring of the chase. She opened the door to another building and stepped inside.

A few moments later Craig reached the door and entered too. She had vanished. He began searching the rooms one by one. There were gold numbers on the wooden doors as if the building was a motel in its past. The yellow doors and white walls each had a dingy hue to them and the hallway was narrow and long.

The search team came, in a few moments, behind Craig. While Craig explored down the drab hallway, the search team began checking each room behind him.

All of the sudden, Craig heard a tinkle like glass to his right. He quickly went into the room and saw a busted window that she had gone through and her blackly dressed image on the outside of the building.

Immediately, Craig rushed out to grab her before something dreadful happened. He cut himself on the pointy glass as he made his hasty exit, but it did not deter him.

He began racing after her. She was headed directly for a mailbox he noticed.

Craig was catching up to her quicker than before. He was within twenty yards of her when she reached the mailbox. She began looking underneath and unstrapped an electronic device that was hidden there. She had to set the controls for the detonation.

Craig noticed, as he neared her, that she was sitting on the ground, shaking her hands furiously as she waited for a response from the device. He knew that she was setting the controls and that he only had a few moments.

He reached down and grabbed the device as he reached her position. She immediately tried to run, but her sitting position made her vulnerable to Craig's controlling arms.

"No you don't, dear," Craig said authoritatively. Relinquishing his arm control and subsequently pointing his pistol at her, he said, "Don't get up."

Motioning one of the security people to come, Craig waited patiently. When they arrived he said, "Don't let this one get out of your sight people." Backing away and turning around, Craig headed for his shuttle.

Inside the complex, were all sorts of people running around, laser fire, blockades, etc. Ben was among the fighting personnel. He was not on the forefront, but instead back behind several men. They had been doing excellent at all attack and fortification points up until now and with minimum casualties too.

The defense forces at this point were starting to firm. They were at attack point 3 and Ben figured this to be their last stand. Their casualties, he thought, were very high. He and his troops, along with all other departments, had taken them completely by surprise.

"Let's try to figure a way around this mess," Ben said to a Platoon Commander Jim Howard.

They both studied the floorplan that Ben unfolded on the command table very carefully. "How about if we go down this hallway and intersect this hallway; then we could have half of fortification point 1, which is not seeing much action, come to this position," Ben suggested.

Pointing to the adjoining hallway, Jim said, "That hallway is more heavily fortified than we are here. I don't really see any alternate but to move some troops from fortification position 1 to here and see if we can't force our way through."

"I suppose you're right," Ben said, "but I don't like it." Grabbing at the communication device on his wrist, Ben set the encryption frequency necessary to talk to fortification point 1. "Calling Platoon Commander Nelson."

"Nelson here, sir."

"Are you still under a light attack commander?"

"Yes, sir."

"Then please send some of your troops to attack point 3," Ben ordered.

"Right away, sir."

The fighting continued in front of Ben while the refresher troops were on their way. The hallways of the whole building were practically demolished. Burn marks from lasers were everywhere. Combat was not a pretty sight, but sometimes it was necessary.

Ben began checking in with the other attack and fortification points. All was going extremely well. All the other points were giving up ground by the yards. Ben's checking in was disturbed by a young ensign.

"Ensign Lin reporting as ordered, sir."

"You and your men take positions," Ben said.

"Yes, sir."

The young men spread out down the hallway, like an octopus spreading its tentacles. The extra men seemed to intimidate their opponents as they started moving in back of their barricades. Back, back, back, they went.

The Orion's members, advancing slowly and carefully, moved down the hallway using their black blast shields for protection. They went past the barricades, and walked down the hallway, being careful to avoid the many bodies and guns on the floor. They moved so far down the hallway that they could see the opening to the Great Room that was in center of the complex, directly under the tower.

Unfortunately, they did not keep on going. The Orion's men could see all kinds of tables and equipment in the room so they knew this was to be a final stand.

Ben, who had been following the assault team, could tell by the few opponents left that this position was virtually conquered and started calling the other teams. All the other teams were continuing to have success as well, but none of them were this close to breaking through.

While Ben was checking with the others, the team of men broke through to the room. Immediately, he cut off his communications, grabbed his laser pistol, and headed into the room.

When he got in the doorway, he saw the many men and women of the Pak, Cartier, Maggie Rem, and Matt. They all had their hands in the air, and were willing to surrender.

Matt said, "Listen ………"

"Not a word," Ben said, pointing his pistol at Matt with a furious sense of betrayal. "Cuff them all," he said to Platoon Commander Howard.

"Wait a minute," said a big, dark haired man.

"What's your problem," Ben asked.

The man said, "I need to talk to your commander."

"What about," asked Ben curiously.

"I'll discuss that with him," the big man said.

"Tell me, why should I let you talk to our most valuable officer," Ben asked with an arrogance.

"The question is," the man said, "can you afford not to. I can tell you valuable things."

What the man said was not that important to Ben, what he wasn't saying was more of value. Ben thought about what was said for several minutes. He could be just a crook who was trying to weasel his way out of a jam, but he could have information on some other stuff too. "All right, wise guy, come with me. You better have something good to say. Think hard."

Craig had barely gotten back aboard the Orion when news of capturing the main headquarters was announced on the ship's intercom. There was a resounding barrage of 'Hooray's' and 'Yay's' from every corner and cranny aboard the vessel. Craig couldn't help but say his own cheer too. The calamity had came and passed with a big bang and the sounds of the cheers indicated what a relief it was for it be over.

Craig walked out of the shuttle bay with a new outlook on people, as if the whole incident changed him in many ways. The walls of the ship could not contain his love of life. He also liked the love of command and responsibility. Few men could have felt his enormous sense of freedom at this juncture.

As he approached the bridge, he couldn't bear the thought of giving up his rank. He had grown quite attached to it, he couldn't see where they would strip it from him, but they may.

The bridge seemed very busy as he walked in. They were coordinating last efforts to put the small, isolated groups down. Busy, busy, busy............

Melanie interrupted his thoughts by saying, "Commander, you're wanted in the ship's brig."

"Thank you. Tell them I'll be right down," Craig responded.

Steadily, Craig marched back into the elevator and went to the brig on one of the bottom decks. He was curious as to what could demand his presence there. He was going to go down and talk to Matt eventually though. He would take care of that while he was there. Knowing that Valerie was too hurt to speak to him, he would say something on behalf of her and the entire crew.

Walking into the brig was harder than he had expected. Although the forcefields held the prisoners in, he did not expected the swarms of medical personnel attending to some of the prisoners. They were dirty and altogether unsightly.

"Commander," Ben shouted from the end of the slender hallway, near a service access door.

"Coming Ben," Craig said as Ben's voice got his attention. When he neared the cubicle where Ben was he said, "What's up?"

"This man says he has some valuable information for you. He refuses to talk to anyone else though," Ben said looking disgusted.

Matt looked at the big man and said, "I'm here now. Speak."

The long blonde headed man said, "Come closer and I'll whisper it to you."

Craig leaned his ear near to the forcefield.

"My name is Terrell Brooks. If you'll check with The Alliance you'll find me as the spy that was assigned this mission."

Craig leaned back in astonishment. He turned toward Ben and whispered in his ear, "Would you check with The Alliance for a man named Terrell Brooks. Advise them of our situation and tell them we need a response pronto. If it checks out, bring the keycard to this service corridor."

Ben took off down the main corridor. He ran all the way to the bridge. Ran the communication through and ran all the way back.

"Here it is commander," Ben said as handed the portable data recorder to him.

"Open that service access corridor Ben. Then get this man out of here. I'll meet you both, and Frank, on the bridge in a few minutes," Craig said.

While Ben and Terrell Brooks made a hasty exit from the brig, Craig walked down to where Matt was. "Matt," he called out.

Matt, straightened his uniform as he stood up. "Craig…" he nearly shouted.

"Yes, it's me Matt," Craig said as Matt approached the forcefield. "Matt, I just wanted to ask you why you turned against the patrol, honesty, laws that you've upheld many times, the people you work with who were your friends, in short virtually everything that you've held dear for years. The people here don't understand it and I don't either."

"Well Craig, I just got caught up in a lust for my dreams. I've always respected the Alliance and Space Patrol, but somehow when I got to my dream position, captain of the Orion, it wasn't what I thought it would be."

"What the hell did you think it was," Craig asked accusingly.

"I was more in love with the ceremonial things that came with the job; like the honors, medals, and respect of all you survey."

"I guess being in power would do that for you, huh?"

Matt was puzzled, "Power, no. After a phony agreement was met through Peter Topper, who only regained his memory two days ago, I would destroy the Orion and load the freighter in orbit around Delta 12 with Alphorzia and sell it somewhere."

"But that ship belonged to Kamon Freights," Craig said with a high pitch.

"Kamon Freights is a dummy company that was recently sold to I-Port Enterprises which is in the Pak's region of space. I paid off someone to destroy the data trail that led to the Pak," Matt explained.

"Well, you caused a lot of problems for me and every other crew member. There's people that are going to be grappling with this for years, both here and in the command center of Star Patrol," Craig said.

"I know. I'm truly sorry. I wish I wouldn't have done it."

"Too late now," Craig said. Matt started to say something, but Craig walked off before he could.

Craig quickly made his way to the bridge all the while thinking about Matt. 'He was a good man,' Craig thought. 'He just made a series of terrible mistakes.' At least Craig thought Matt was good. How can you have that many good times, that many bad, and experience your life with a person for that long of a period, without ever really knowing that person?

He supposed it meant he should never underestimate anyone, but Craig wondered about loved ones, women, children… Don't you know them?

He had always been a believer in people. The strength of one's character was shown in the building of a relationship with them, he believed. But this incident made him realize that people only show a certain side of themselves to you. That side was reflective in the way you act towards them. Craig thought, 'No one can truly know another.' He would put that philosophy into practice in his everyday dealings with people.

When the turbovator door opened, Craig immediately saw Frank in the command chair. Mister Brooks was standing to the left of the chair and the rest of the bridge crew were busily coordinating efforts to get Delta III's governing body into effective positions so that they could operate.

"Hello all," said Craig with a smile on his face as he stepped through the doors of the turbovator.

Frank turned his head to greet Craig. "Hello Craig. Melanie, contact Central Command."

"Yes, sir." Melanie started pushing buttons and in a moment said, "Admiral Rutherford on the screen, sir."

The image of the grayish man in his 50's appeared on the screen once more. This was the moment that Craig had worried about since he was made acting commander. Would they strip him of his title?

"This is Acting Commander Holt here, sir. We would like to advise you of some new developments."

The admiral said, "I know of the situation, acting commander. It's was lucky Terrell could get a transmission to you."

"Then you know about Matthew Roberts, sir," Craig said questioningly.

"Yes, I do. It's a terrible thing to have happen. It forces us to examine our ongoing screening procedures, and the whole way in which we treat our members. We can not allow this to happen again," Admiral Rutherford said.

"Yes. It's terrible," Craig said.

The admiral's face showed no emotion when he said, "As far your replacement personnel, I have been considering all possibilities."

'Oh no. Here it comes,' thought Craig.

"I have been looking at the records of all available candidates for the rank of captain as well as thinking about your temporary rank of commander. It appears to me, Mister Holt, that your conduct during this crisis was exemplary and due to your former commanders lack of experience, I am promoting you to the rank of captain. You may promote, at your discretion, people to the missing positions from within your crew's compliment.

"Craig, it is the view of myself and others in Central Command that you've grown out of your young, foolish ways. May you forever live up to our expectations," the heartfelt admiral said.

Elated, Craig said exuberantly, "I will, sir, very much. And thank you."

"Rutherford out." The screen blank went as the prideful joy that Craig felt escalated to fill every inch of his body. The takeover was quick and was to last a long time. The emotions overwhelmed him. He had long ago dismissed this possibility in his lifetime.

"Frank," Craig said with pride.

"Yes, captain," Frank said using Craig's new rank as a form of respect.

"You are hereby promoted, or rather reestablished as commander," Craig said overflowing with happiness. "Your first assignment is to find a general science officer."

"I think Lieutenant Ravek would be a good choice," Frank said.

"I think so too," Craig replied.

Hitting the button on the intercom on the arm of the command chair, Craig said, "Captain to Lieutenant Reaton."

Jane, in the computer center, knew Craig's voice, but captain? She was so proud for him. "Reaton here Captain Holt."

"Please meet at the restaurant Monamie in 10 minutes dear."

"Happy to oblige, Captain Holt."

Craig looked at Frank and said, "If you need me commander I'll be at Monamie's."

Craig left the bridge in favor of the restaurant. The ship had a different feel to it. It was as if the ship had been reborn. The circulated air seemed fresher; the ship seemed cleaner; the crew seemed more alert.

Thinking about the crew made him think of how they would react to his being promoted. He had been on the Orion a long time, perhaps longer than anyone else. He knew almost everyone aboard ship. He thought the longer he commanded, the more they would trust him.

Of course anyone would have a tough time at first. After all, this crew was betrayed by the last captain. But, as time went by, they would come to trust him too. Obeying orders was essential for any chain of command to operate. That's what caused the situation with Matt, disobedience to his oath.

Jane had beaten him to the restaurant. She already had a table ready for the two of them. There were drinks in place, table settings, and menu's sitting on the table.

"Howdy Ho, Captain," Jane said.

"Hello, lovely one," replied Craig with a smile. He pulled out the chair that was across from hers and began to seat himself."

"So tell me all the sorted details."

Craig spent several minutes telling her about the events of the day. He couldn't help but smile at the end of his story.

"It's a dream come true for me," Craig said.

"I know it is, honey. What do you intend on doing for the next few days," Jane asked.

"Well, we've got to reestablish the controlling government here. While that's going on we can start clean up efforts and processing of the criminals. Other than that, just get the lone freighter back to a shipyard."

"I see."

"I tell you, Jane, I don't know if I can be any happier," Craig said with confidence.

Jane leaned forward and put her arms around Craig's neck. He, in return, put his arms around her neck. As they passionately kissed each other enduringly, Craig could not believe what he felt. That did make it better.

***

About This Author

Mark Wayne Allen was born in Merryville, Louisiana. He has a Bachelor of Science degree in business from Louisiana State University and was trained in computers at Louisiana Tech University. Despite being a quadriplegic, he remains very active in life and in the community.

He has written a number of works, fiction, poetry, and non-fiction.

*

Keep in touch with the author at http://markwayneallen.com

Coming soon...
MELVIN TIME

www.ingramcontent.com/pod-product-compliance
Lightning Source LLC
Chambersburg PA
CBHW050036180626
46810CB00002B/738